Unraveled

By

Elizabeth Castle

Name: Castle, Elizabeth, author

Title: Unraveled

Description: Series: The Cantwell Quartet

Publisher: In The Air Publishing

Identifiers: ISBN 9781967731220 (ebook) | ISBN 9781967731237 (paperback) | ISBN 9798305270464 (amazon hardcover)

Cover Design by betibup33

Chapter One

Trenton Armstrong whistled while he worked. Today was a good day. Last night, two of his best friends had gotten married. And to each other. Gideon Eginhard was as steady as they came. Penny Camhion, now Eginhard, was soft and sweet, yet strong. The perfect foil for Gideon.

He could still picture the look on Penny's face when he showed up at her parents' house for the wedding with a pair of antique tables for their bedroom. For some reason, a reason that made Penny blush, the pair had moved Gideon's bed from his apartment to her house and then decided to redecorate the master bedroom. Since it was still mostly empty, he figured the tables were the perfect gift. Gideon had eyed the tables as if he thought something might pop out of them. Trenton had laughed. It had been years since any gift he'd given exploded. Though there had been some memorable ones over the years. But this was a wedding. Serious business. So no games, no jokes. He wished the pair the best and was glad Penny loved the tables.

Penny's love of antiques was one of the passions they shared. He and Penny had been friends and companions for a lot of years. But the two of them had never been attracted to each other. Trenton had known, even when Gideon was denying it, that his friend was in love with Penny. That made her off-limits, even if the attraction had been there.

Trenton watched the stock numbers scroll by. Numbers had always been his specialty. Nash Camhion, who was almost as good with numbers as he was, was the better poker player and gambler. Trenton knew never to gamble with anything important, and for Trenton, money was one of the most important things. When one had none, making more once you did could become an obsession.

Trenton rose and stretched. His eye caught the shine from a photo frame, and he walked to the bookcase where it sat. The quartet. He loved these men with every fiber of his being. Two blonds, two brunettes. Four men, four brothers, though not by blood. But they shared a bond unlike anything he had known in his early years. He'd do anything for his brothers. He'd die for them.

Nash Camhion was the leader. The Prince, as Gideon, the second member of the quartet, liked to call him. All teeth and charm. Women were drawn to him like flies to honey. His smoky black hair, athletic build, and endless charm attracted women of all ages. There had been a memorable occasion when an eighty-year-old woman had pinched his butt and tucked her number down the front of his pants. Nash had smiled at her, told her she was a doll, and somehow managed to get himself out of the situation without offending the woman. By the time he'd walked away, she'd been blushing like a teenager.

But Nash had a dark side. The demons in his past were many. He'd been kidnapped when he'd been thirteen. His grandfather, Cormac Camhion, had died trying to protect his grandson. He'd died lying in the street while Nash had been taken. Nash never told his family the whole truth of what had happened. The sanitized version of events had been bad enough. The truth was worse. Nash had been sixteen when he'd finally broken. He'd told the quartet all of the horrific things he'd suffered at the hands of his captor. The rest of the quartet held him as he shed painful tears, each of them shedding their own in camaraderie and in pain at what their friend had gone through.

Gideon Eginhard, he was the protector. The Sword, as Trenton liked to call him. He was the one who had saved Nash from the kidnapper. He bore two large scars in a cross pattern over his right eye. One gash ran from above his eyebrow down to his cheek. The other ran across his forehead. Gideon had snuck out late that night, intending to commit his first act of robbery. Instead, he'd saved a boy his own age from being killed and turned his life to the path of right. He was now a cop and a newly promoted detective. And now he was married to Nash's little sister, Penny.

Isaac Brandt was the third member of the quartet. He was the brains. He was the one you could trust to bring peace and logic to any situation. Some people thought he was boring. Some said stodgy. Trenton might have thought the same if he didn't know him so well. Isaac was the son of a prominent diplomat. His father spoke a dozen languages and held two peace prizes, though not the Nobel he coveted. But the fact that the man bullied his own son never came to light. In retaliation, Isaac surpassed his father. He spoke fifteen languages, could read twenty, and had more doctorate degrees than Trenton could count. Isaac rarely spoke to his father and had no plans to change it. When they did happen to cross paths, usually through university functions, Isaac extricated himself as soon as possible.

Isaac was probably the only one who didn't have a dark past. One would say he was least like the others. But his level-headedness brought balance to the group. Trenton liked to think he was the glue that held them all together. And best of all, the man could cook.

Trenton, well, he was the goofball. The funny guy. At least that was how he was perceived by outsiders. And how he wanted to be perceived. He had been the last to join the quartet. He was two years younger than the rest of them, who were all in the same grade. Isaac had been tasked with tutoring him. Isaac saw something in him, and he had taken a young Trenton under his wing. After Trenton met Nash and Gideon, Trenton had a pretty good idea of what Isaac saw. There was something dark lurking under the surface of the other two boys. The guys had befriended him, and before he knew it, he'd become part of the group.

Trenton's phone buzzed, and he turned from the photograph. He saw Isaac's name on the screen. Of the four, Trenton was still closest to Isaac. "Hey, what's up? Didn't get enough of me at the wedding?"

Isaac ignored the comment. "I got an odd message from a journalist. She has written a few biographies and has interviewed some important people. She's asking for an interview with me."

Isaac was not only a professor at Georgetown, but he was also a successful author. Between his historical books on peace treaties and foreign wars and his growing works in science fiction and fantasy, it wasn't surprising. "So, what, you need me to dazzle her for you?"

Isaac scoffed. "I don't think I'm interested in dazzling her. Impress her, perhaps. But she read the article Nash published and saw the interviews he's been giving about Cantwell. I was surprised she would know anything about the gaming industry, given she's a biographer, but she said she'd love to not only talk to me about my body of work but also to interview all of us as a side story."

Trenton thought about it. "What's her name?"

"Ginny Page."

Trenton whistled. "Didn't she interview a president?"

Isaac couldn't hide his surprise that he knew the name. "You never cease to amaze me. But yeah. Not ours. She has interviewed a few prominent political figures in Washington. D.C, I believe. I was surprised because she's so young, but she became an instant bestseller when she wrote her first book. So what do you think?"

Trenton was not playing dumb. "Think about what?"

Isaac sighed. "Letting her interview me. I can't imagine why me of all people. I thought she could come to Cantwell's office and see what we're up to. It would be great publicity if nothing else. But everyone would need to be on board."

Trenton couldn't help it. "My ever-practical friend. I think that if Ginny Page wants to interview you, you say 'yes, please.' She's brilliant. Not as brilliant as you are, but maybe a close second."

Isaac's hum came over the line. "All right. I'll answer her call. Just seems odd."

Trenton didn't like the shiver that went up his back. "What could possibly be odd? You're smart, you have a new book coming out, you have two cool jobs, and you're not a bad-looking guy."

Isaac hummed again. "I have three jobs."

Trenton was so glad he took the bait. "Yeah, but you're the most boring teacher I've ever heard."

Isaac gave a third hum. "Delilah would agree with you."

Trenton felt bad. Delilah, or Lilah as she preferred, had become a sore spot for Isaac. "I'm just kidding. She doesn't know you the way we do. Though we all know you're sweet on her. You should show her your fun side."

Isaac was quiet for a moment. "I don't have a fun side. But I'll take that under advisement. I've got to go. I'm guest lecturing at the university today for a colleague."

Trenton hung up. Sometimes Isaac made him feel like he'd kicked a puppy. Isaac's problem was that he spent too much time with his head in a book. Lilah was gorgeous under her baggy clothes and wavy red hair. Trenton thought her freckles were adorable. Like Gideon with Penny, Trenton could tell Isaac was attracted to her. So he and Lilah had a platonic relationship, one where they simply discussed work, photography, and money.

Speaking of, Trenton went back to his computer. Lilah was his first client now that he was freelancing. He'd worked for an investment firm for years. He grew his own portfolio twenty-fold over the years. And he'd made the firm a ton, too. But he'd learned to hate sitting at his desk in the overly decorated office day after day. Only his frequent travels kept him sane. When that was no longer enough to stop his restlessness, he knew he had to get out before it drove him mad. He was finding that helping others was more fulfilling than making his rich clients richer.

Lilah's mom was sick, and Trenton had offered to help. He'd found Lilah crying in the bathroom. He hadn't meant to pry, but the gut-wrenching tears she had been trying to stifle were more than his heart could handle. After much coaxing, Lilah admitted her mother was sick and that she was struggling to pay the bills. The doctor had prescribed a very expensive medication that was beyond Lilah's ability to pay. Trenton had helped her wash her face and asked her how much money she had. Lilah had been about to brush him off, but he'd promised to double her investment. An easy promise, given she only had a couple hundred dollars left to her name, and that was after getting paid. Two weeks later he'd come back with a check. Shyly she'd asked him if he could do it again. And he had. In return, Lilah had poured herself into the Cantwell project and had been working more hours than any of them. He did keep it to himself that he'd padded the account. All of the quartet had. Lilah had become an instrumental part of the team.

Cantwell. Trenton picked up the book that lay on his desk. Isaac really was a genius. Cantwell was Isaac's first foray into fantasy and romance. Nash had read the book and immediately came up with a game concept. Within a very short time, Cantwell had been formed. They'd all kicked in equal amounts of money. Gideon, being a cop, didn't have as much money as the rest of them. But Trenton had been building his portfolio, and Gideon had put the whole sum in. Each of them then matched it.

Trenton went to his bookcase and pulled out a book on the actress Sonny Madison. The biography had been Ginny

Page's first book. It probably hadn't hurt that Sonny had just starred in a movie that had grossed triple-digit millions. The book Ginny had written on the actress had made the bestseller list in less than two weeks after it hit stores. Trenton wasn't particularly interested in Sonny Madison, though he did enjoy her movies. It was the author who intrigued him.

Trenton flipped the book over. A subtly pretty brunette stared back at him. Like Lilah, she had a sprinkling of freckles on her face that made her appear young, though he figured she was probably older than she looked. There was a maturity in her writing that lent itself to an older, more experienced person. There was not much information about the author on the book jacket. In fact, there was very little about her on the internet. He'd looked.

Trenton's phone rang. This time it was Nash. "Hey. How are you holding up?"

Nash's tapping on the case of his phone came over the line. "You know I'm ecstatic. About time, I swear. I'm just glad they didn't push it out and just did the deed. But I just got off the phone with Isaac. That's amazing news. Gideon is a fan of Ginny Page's books, too. Isaac didn't call him, but he'll be pumped when he finds out. What do you think?"

Trenton gazed down at the book jacket. "I think Isaac deserves some recognition for his books. And when Cantwell hits the bookstores after the game is released, he's going to be more famous than he realizes. Poor guy won't know what to do with that kind of attention."

"No kidding. At least he's not as shy as he used to be."

Trenton dropped back into his desk chair. "So hard to

remember how we all were years ago. I think we all turned out all right."

Nash made a humming sound, not unlike Isaac. "I've been thinking about it a lot. Hard not to after what happened. I won't mind getting back to work now that all the wedding hoopla is over. I could use a distraction. And Ginny Page looks like a nice distraction, if you ask me."

Trenton wanted to tell him no one asked him, but he realized how absurd that would sound. And Nash's tone hadn't gotten past him. "If you want to hang out, I'm free. Or if you want to talk about anything."

The line was silent for a moment. Then Nash finally spoke. "I am still having a hard time about Clara. It's been easy with the wedding for all of us to pretend it didn't happen. But Dad has been talking to Hayden, and I don't like it. I want to put all of this behind us."

Trenton agreed. The past two months since Clara was killed had been hard for the Camhion family. Someone had tried to kidnap Penny. Thankfully Penny had gotten away. At least the first time. It had brought up painful memories for the entire Camhion clan. It then came to light that Clara, Penny and Nash's cousin, was the one behind the kidnapping. She had tried to kill both of them. She'd torched Cantwell's headquarters with Nash inside in an attempt to burn Nash alive. Instead of leaving Penny in the building to die in the blaze, Clara had taken her with the intent to kill her in Penny's home. But Gideon had put the pieces together and found Penny in time. In the end, Clara was dead; shot by Gideon.

Trenton didn't push. He rubbed a spot on his chest.

Sometimes a man just needed to be alone. "I'm around if you want to pop over. I've got lots of frozen pizza and beer. And I'm just working on my business plan. Though I can't seem to find any enthusiasm for it right now."

"I'm going to take a raincheck. Penny and Gideon should be on an airplane right now. Mom and Dad are ready to call it a day. Mom's exhausted. I'm going to crash at my parents' house tonight. I stuck around and helped with the cleanup. We can meet up in the morning at Cantwell. Isaac will probably need us to convince him to call Ginny Page back. No doubt he'll change his mind a dozen times tonight while he tries to figure out all possible outcomes of whether he agrees or not."

Trenton couldn't help but smile at that. "We all know him so well. But we can talk him into it, and then have him work on the storyboards with me. If we don't nail down the rest of the story, Lilah might go rogue again."

Nash made a hissing noise. "That woman. She's lucky she's so good at her job. We've argued for the past four days over your last boards."

Trenton felt no sympathy. "And yet she has won almost every one of those arguments, even though you're the boss. Women. Go figure."

Nash relented. "Okay, yes, she's usually right once I see it. How is her portfolio going, by the way?"

Trenton pulled up the numbers and told him. "Not bad for starters. Her mom is going to need a lot of care. I figure her portfolio will keep me busy while I continue to work on my client list. Some of my previous clients from the firm have already reached out to me."

"It's because you're too good at what you do. That ridiculously large house you live in is proof of that. It's bigger than mine."

Trenton glanced around. The house was way more than a man like him needed. No wife, no kids. No family, outside of the quartet and an aunt and uncle who had taken him in when his mom died. Thanks to them, he'd gone to the private school that Nash, Gideon, and Isaac attended. If for nothing else, he owed them for that. But he owed the quartet much more than he could ever repay.

Nash's phone beeped. "Gotta go. Lilah is texting me pictures again. That woman needs to get some sleep. She works more than we do."

Trenton tapped a couple of keys and put a little more money into her account. "Sometimes work can help you keep your mind off your troubles, right? So I figure as long as she doesn't push herself too hard, I won't complain. No worse than either of us on our bad days."

Nash concurred. "All right. I won't tell her to go to bed. Though it's tempting. I'll go over these with her tomorrow. You can come and referee."

"I'll be there with a chair and a whip."

* * *

Across town, Gentiana Lucinda Page-Hamlin, professionally known as Ginny Page, checked her email for the dozenth time. She had emailed Isaac Brandt last week, and she hadn't heard back from him. While he would make for an interesting book, that wasn't why she wanted to interview him. If he didn't respond soon, she was going to go find him. She had never had a prospective interviewee not respond to her right away. Her name meant something these days, and having her interview them could be just the boost their careers needed. Not that Isaac really needed her help, but she was not going to tell him that.

Ginny pushed her pin-straight brunette hair out of her face. She'd spent the last hour pacing the hotel room she was staying in. She wasn't a patient person on a good day. And today was not one of her better days. She'd gotten no response to a few discreet inquiries she'd made. She wanted more information before she went into the lion's den. Or in this case, Cantwell's headquarters.

Ginny went to the window that overlooked the packed parking lot. She never stayed in fancy hotels. She didn't like drawing attention to herself. And despite most of her books gracing bestseller lists, she still was able to keep a low profile. It probably helped that she preferred print over television. She stayed off social media. And as much as possible, she kept cameras off of her. Even the photo on her books was an outdated shot that was taken more than five years ago when she'd had short hair and worn glasses all the time. Today she kept her hair long and her contacts in.

On the desk sat files on all four men who comprised Cantwell.

Nash Camhion. Now that one was a pretty boy, no doubt. She thought herself immune to his kind of charm. He was not a low-profile person. The man had modeled for a time, was part of an extremely wealthy family, and wasn't shy in front of cameras.

Gideon Eginhard. Now he was an intense-looking man. No doubt he would dwarf her five-foot-three-inch frame. He was over six feet. She knew he was a detective with the local police department and that he had a reputation as a good cop. Ginny couldn't help but sarcastically wonder where the honest cops were when she needed them? In her mind, the only good cop was one that hadn't gotten caught yet.

Dr. Isaac Brant. His books were brilliant. She was an admirer of his work. She was looking forward to interviewing him. Assuming he emailed her back. He held multiple doctorates, but his passion was writing. Ginny could relate to that. Cantwell was a departure for him, so it intrigued her how he went from non-fiction, academic works to science fiction, fantasy, and romance in under four years. Ginny had written a couple of fiction book, sweet romance novels meant for teens, but she knew her true talent lay in non-fiction.

Trenton Armstrong. He was her true target. On the surface, he was a successful financial advisor and investor. In reality, he was much more. She wanted all of his secrets.

Ginny stopped pacing and grabbed her cell phone. She dialed the only person she wanted to talk to right now. "Hi. Can you put Gwenny on the phone?"

A soft, excited voice came over the line. "Hi, Mommy."

Ginny's pinched lips turned into a smile, and the tension of her day faded. "Hi, sweetie. How was school today?"

Ginny listened as Gwenny told her all about her day. But when Gwenny once again mentioned the man in black, Ginny shivered. "Put Levi back on the phone. I love you.

And I hope to see you very soon."

"Yes." Levi responded in his usual one-word replies.

"Any luck?"

"No."

"Did you see him?"

"No."

Ginny hit "end" on her phone. She needed to find the man in black. And soon.

Chapter Two

Ginny knocked on the front door of the lovely brick home on a residential street. A very well-to-do neighborhood. She had spent hours trying to find Cantwell's office. The first address had been a burned-down and condemned building across town. A very undesirable part of town, she might add. This looked better, but perhaps not more promising. The men who owned Cantwell could certainly own a home in this neighborhood. Perhaps not the cop, but her recent research showed he married Penelope Camhion, heiress to a fortune. And the sister of Cantwell's founding partner, Ignatius "Nash" Camhion.

Ginny had been debating for days whether she should surprise them or wait until Dr. Brandt contacted her again with a date, but as of yet, he had not reached out, except to say he would let her know when it would be convenient to meet. Ginny's patience had run out. And she wasn't going to be deterred, certainly not when she was this close to the man she had been searching for.

She knocked a few times, and when no one answered, she wandered around the property. She didn't see another entrance.

"Ma'am, you're trespassing on private property." A large man with scars on his face popped his head out of the top-floor window.

Ginny was startled for a moment and then calmed her breathing. Gideon Eginhard. The police detective. He seemed much larger in person. His police employment record stated he was thirty-eight years old and a newly promoted detective.

She took a step back so that he could get a better look at her. She didn't want to get on this man's bad side. "Sorry for the intrusion. I knocked, but no one answered. I was looking for another entrance. I'm Ginny Page."

The dark-haired man's eyes narrowed. "I don't recall inviting you."

Ginny gave him her best reporter's smile. "I realize that. But I was hoping that you'd forgive the intrusion."

Another head popped out the window. Nash Camhion. He was hard to miss. The man was ridiculously attractive. His hair was longer than the pictures she had of him. The hair was grey-black, and she knew his eyes were the color of smoke. He had been the easiest to find. After years of having his face plastered on fashion magazines, he'd become a major player in the social scene of Washington D.C. There probably wasn't a beautiful woman in town he hadn't been seen with. Or rather, them being seen with him.

"Ms. Page, I'm sure it's a pleasure. But no one is allowed inside Cantwell's offices."

Ginny kept her smile on her face. "How about a living room or parlor?"

A third voice cursed. Nash's face disappeared to be replaced by Dr. Isaac Brandt. "I told you I would contact you when I was ready."

She knew he would likely be the one to be swayed. "I

realize that. However, I've been anxious to meet you. And I have a deadline. I know you, of all people, can empathize with deadlines."

All the heads disappeared. She was disappointed when Trenton's face didn't appear after his friends. She sincerely hoped he was here. She hadn't spent the past year and a half trying to find him only to have him elude her.

Isaac's face reappeared. "I'll be down."

When his face disappeared, so did her smile. Shrewd eyes scanned the area as she made her way back to the front door. The book on Dr. Brandt would be a feather in her cap. He was on his way up, no doubt. There was a nerdy charm to him; he was tall and lean, and handsome enough to attract women. He was smart, well-read, and, she hoped, charming. But even if he wasn't, she knew how to spin a story.

The front door opened, and her smile returned. "I really appreciate your allowing me to intrude."

Isaac eyed her. She knew she wasn't as impressive in person as she was in print. She always wished she had another five inches, but such was not her lot. Her brown hair was pin straight, but with rollers and a lot of hair product, she managed to get some body and waves in it. She was slender, which was in her favor, but she didn't have the curves men seemed so attracted to. She kept her makeup light and natural instead of going for bombshell, but she usually was able to charm a man into ignoring her physical shortcomings.

"I'm not sure this is the best place to meet for an interview."

Ginny relaxed as he let her in. "Oh, I wasn't going to interview you today. I just wanted to get a lay of the land, so to speak. And you did say that Mr. Camhion had agreed to talk to me about Cantwell. I am hoping the other members are also willing to chat with me. I got my hands on an advanced copy of your book. It's a beautiful story."

Isaac cursed. It seemed strange for a man who looked so scholarly. "And how exactly, Ms. Page, did you manage that? The book is not supposed to be available until the game is released, which isn't until next year."

Ginny's eyes tightened, but her smile didn't waver. "I apologize if I overstepped my bounds. Your agent was happy to give me a copy when I met with him."

Ginny left out the part where she had to spend an hour sucking up to him, telling him what a wonderful agent he was and how brilliant he was. Enough compliments, and he'd been eating out of the palm of her hand. And while she'd managed to get her hands on the physical copy of the book before he had agreed to give it to her, she had managed to get him to agree to it after she had already perused a few pages.

"Well?" Isaac's arms crossed over his chest.

"Books take time. By the time my book on you comes out, your game will be released, as will your book. So there is no harm done to the confidentiality of your book before it comes out. I'm known to be a trustworthy reporter."

A tall blond man came down the stairs. His hair was a sunny shade that seemed unusual in a man. He had a broad chest and shoulders and was wearing dress slacks with a dress shirt that was casually unbuttoned at the neck. His face was clean-shaven, and locks of that golden hair fell on his forehead. He was thirty-six, two years younger than his three counterparts. She knew he was five foot eleven. And she was one of the few people who knew where he'd been born.

Trenton came into the room, his eyes on the petite woman still standing in front of the entry door. "Good afternoon, Ms. Page. This is a surprise."

She was staring. She knew she was, but she couldn't seem to unlock her gaze from his. Then suddenly, she snapped out of it. "Mr. Armstrong, correct?"

He gave her a flirtatious smile. "Yes. You can call me Trenton."

She unconsciously returned the smile. "I'm glad that all of you are here. I was hoping to be able to introduce myself to everyone. Again, my apologies for intruding."

Nash and Gideon followed behind Trenton.

Nash came and held out a hand. "Well, Ms. Page, you have all of us."

She popped her reporter smile back on, even though her heart was pounding in her chest. "A handsome bunch, if I may say so. Female readers, and a few men, will be thrilled."

Nash kept her hand in his. He lifted it for a moment to his lips. "And you're quite charming, Ms. Page."

Ginny let him hold her hand for a moment before extracting it. She then held her hand out to Isaac. "You can all call me Ginny. I am very happy to meet you, Dr. Brandt."

Isaac took her hand. "I suppose we'll see."

She then held her hand to Gideon, who was watching her with critical eyes. Her smile slipped for a moment. "I hear congratulations are in order. I heard about your promotion when I read about you in the papers."

Gideon held her hand, his eyes probing. "Thank you. It was an honor."

She was relieved when he let her go. She took a deep breath and held her hand out to Trenton. "And I'm glad to meet you as well."

Trenton took her hand. Unlike the other three handshakes, the contact made her hand tremble in his. Both dropped their hands simultaneously, as if shocked. Her eyes widened for a moment before remembering what she was supposed to be doing here.

Trenton pulled his gaze away, walked to the stairs, and yelled. "Lilah, you should probably come down, too."

A mumble came from upstairs before a tall, slender redhead with long hair, violet eyes, and very baggy clothes came down the stairs in a pair of striped socks.

Nash took her hand as she came down the stairs. "This is our computer whiz, Delilah Fitzpatrick."

Ginny thought the gesture was protective, almost paternal. She then noticed the slight limp in the woman's gait. She held her hand out to the young woman. "Nice to meet you. I didn't see anything in the press about a fifth partner."

Lilah shook her head. "No, I'm not a partner. They hired me to help with some of the development and graphics for the game."

Trenton flanked her. "I think you should interview her, too. She'll be extremely flattering about all of us. Well, except Isaac, maybe."

"Shut up, Trenton." Isaac scowled at his friend.

Trenton held up a hand. "I swear to tell the truth, the whole truth."

Lilah stifled a giggle. "It's nice to meet you, anyway. These four will give you a run for your money. And I'm happy to help with your book if everyone else is okay with me talking to you. But excuse me for now; I'm in the middle of something."

Isaac's eyes followed her up the stairs. "She hates it when we interrupt her."

Trenton nudged him. "You mean when you interrupt her. But I digress." Serious eyes turned to Ginny. "So, why Isaac?"

Ginny almost tripped over her lies; his eyes were so intense. There was more to this man than he had originally shown her. She opted for the part of the truth she could share. "I'm a fan of Dr. Brandt's work. History fascinates me. And he does it very well. His fictional stories take you out of your world and immerse you in his. That takes a lot of talent."

Isaac blushed a bit. "Thank you. So how do you want to do this?"

Ginny tore her eyes from Trenton. "I prefer to interview one at a time. I imagine your story will overlap with the rest of the group's interviews."

Trenton stepped forward. "Let me take you to dinner. We can start with me."

Ginny felt a fluttering in her stomach, one that was not welcome. With her reporter smile back on her face, she spoke. "I'd love to."

* * *

Trenton watched until Ginny was in her car and on her way. He came inside. "Is it just me, or was that strange?"

Nash shrugged. "She could barely take her eyes off of you. So it was probably strange for you. She's got a good reputation. But if you thought that exchange was strange, why did you ask her to dinner?"

Trenton dropped onto the couch. "No clue. I've been a fan of hers since her first book. She wasn't what I was expecting. She was friendly, which I suppose is expected. That fake smile of hers was annoying. But she kept looking at me like she was trying to see inside me. It wasn't an 'I'm attracted to you' look. I don't know what it was. But it was strange."

Isaac sat beside him. "For someone who claims I'm the reason she's in town, it did seem odd she kept looking at you. But maybe that look is her 'I'm attracted to you' look. You seemed to enjoy flirting with her."

Trenton always flirted with the ladies. Perhaps not as much as Nash, but it was a habit. Female attention had been in short supply when he was a teenager. Some of the girls had laughed at him and picked on him. It wasn't until he hit twenty, shot up a few more inches, and started working out in earnest that women started paying attention to him. But he'd been jaded by then and blew all those girls off. He got along with Penny so well because she'd always been kind to him, even as a gangly teenager. There wasn't a mean bone in her body.

Ginny Page was fascinating. He had expected her to be taller, and her picture hadn't done her justice. Her skin had a light bronze tone, and she looked fit. Her skirt had been modest, but he still had noticed the shapely legs beneath the hem. The blouse she wore hadn't clung to her, but he couldn't help but admire her high breasts and trim waist beneath it.

But despite the attraction, it had been strange. It was the only word he could come up with. He couldn't remember a time when a woman had stared at him like that. It was like she was looking at him under a magnifying glass, trying to see inside the man. It was disconcerting. And since Isaac was his best friend, he figured he'd do the same to her before he unleashed her on his friend. Isaac might be capable of taking care of himself, but Trenton had always felt protective of him. Isaac had taken him under his wing, befriended him when he had none, and had been there during the aftermath of the darkest days of his life. Isaac never judged; never offered sympathy. He had simply been there when Trenton had needed him.

Nash stood by the window, his eyes on Trenton. "She's pretty."

Isaac seconded that. "Very. Soft."

Lilah stepped down the last step and had a flush to her skin. "Sorry. Wasn't trying to eavesdrop. She is certainly pretty, though. Isaac, your agent's secretary is on the line upstairs. She said you're not answering your phone again."

Isaac sighed and stood. "I never should have given her the number here. Did she say what Stefan wanted?"

Lilah just stared at him, arms crossed over her chest.

Isaac sighed again. "Yes, I know, you're not my secretary. You answer Nash's calls. And Trenton's. And even Gideon's."

Lilah dropped her arms and moved out of his way. "I answered it, didn't I?"

Voices faded as they went upstairs.

"Isaac is so in love with her. It's painful to see." Nash shook his head.

Gideon glanced at the stairs. "I wish I knew what Delilah's issue is with him. She is closed-mouthed when it comes to him. And she won't let him anywhere near her computer. Her talent is off the charts. Isaac could use her for his graphic novel if he decides to write one."

Nash's eyes took on a determined edge. "Oh, he will."

Trenton had an idea what Lilah's issue was with him, but he kept it to himself. She had reluctantly confided in him, at least part of her reasons, and it wasn't his place to repeat it. "I think she likes him, too."

Nash's smoky brow rose. "She has me fooled. I don't see anything even close to 'like' when she looks at him."

Gideon turned the subject back to Ginny Page. "As far as Ginny goes, I agree with Trent. That was weird."

Nash gazed at his best friend. "I didn't like the way she looked at you."

Gideon wasn't fazed. "It was either the scars or she doesn't like cops."

Trenton interjected. "Or both. But she flipped the switch fast enough."

That hadn't gotten past Gideon, either. "That was the fakest smile I've ever seen. The 'you can trust me' grin that hides a very shrewd mind. I'd watch it with that one."

Nash wasn't worried. "She's harmless. She's got an agenda, no doubt. But so do I. We'll get good press from this. And when her book comes out, we can use that in our marketing, too. We'll get it in writing. I've been working on the contract."

Trenton laughed. "You should have been a lawyer, pretty boy."

Nash's eyes sparked. "I am."

Gideon wagged a finger at him. "Having a law degree is not the same thing as being a lawyer. I don't think your father is ever going to forgive you for not taking the exams."

Nash waved it off. "Can't be a lawyer. We'd be a cliché. You know, the cop and lawyer, friends and enemies."

Isaac came down in the tail end. "You should write a book, Nash. Your imagination is not to be believed sometimes. Or your excuses."

"You're the writer. I'll be the businessman." Nash headed to the stairs. "Am I going to have to calm Lilah down now that you've been talking to her?"

Isaac thought about it. "Probably."

Nash cursed. "Seriously, buddy, you need to work on your people skills."

Trenton leaned back into the cushions. "Don't worry, Isaac, I'll handle your press. By the time I'm done charming Ginny, she'll think you're amazing."

Isaac muttered. "I can't tell if you're serious or teasing."

Trenton shrugged. "Does it matter?"

Gideon and Isaac turned to Trenton with a unanimous "no."

Chapter Three

Ginny was impressed by the restaurant, which was probably the point. The waiter knew Trenton by name and took them to a quiet corner. The lighting was soft, the tables were covered in expensive linen, and there was a string trio playing across the room.

Trenton held Ginny's chair. She glanced back at him. "This is very nice."

Trenton took the seat opposite her. "I'm glad you like it."

Ginny took the folded napkin and laid it in her lap. "Bring all your dates here?"

Trenton handed her a menu. "Not as many as you think."

Ginny heard his serious tone. "I think you mean that."

Trenton opened his menu. "Read all the articles about my playboy ways?"

Ginny sipped her water. "Well, yes, as a matter of fact. Society pages are very active in this town. I found as many mentions of you as I did of your friend, Nash. Sometimes together."

"Nash hates to socialize."

Ginny doubted it. "He's awfully good at it for someone who hates it."

Trenton picked up his water but didn't drink it. "Want to explain how reading the society pages is helping you with your article on Cantwell or your book on Isaac?"

Ginny was used to questions like that. "I like full pictures. And I don't like surprises."

Trenton took a sip. "Who does?"

Ginny changed the subject. "What do you do for Cantwell?"

"Money."

Ginny's annoyance showed. "My article will be very thin if all your answers are one word."

"You've read the book, Ginny. Isaac is the heart. Gideon is the artist. Nash is the designer. And I'm the money. Really simple."

Ginny pulled a tablet out of her purse. With a stylus, she took some notes. "I can start with that. No artistic talent, Trenton?"

Trenton sat back. He slowly looked her over. "My talents lie elsewhere."

With any other man, she'd have stood, told him he was a pig, and stormed out. But Trenton's gaze made her stomach clench, along with other parts of her. She tucked her arms over her chest to cover the sudden beading of her nipples. "Really. You need a better line."

Trenton went back to sipping his water. "I think it worked just fine."

Ginny felt her face flush, but she ignored him and willed her body to relax. She opened and hid behind her menu. She ignored Trenton's satisfied chuckle.

They were quiet while they both studied the menu. By the time the waiter came and took their order and delivered her wine and his sparkling water, she had relaxed.

"So you said no artistic talent. You work as an investment broker. You must have a talent for numbers and computers. So the money. You work for Gregory & Gaines, right?"

"Something you don't know. I quit."

Ginny thought there was a story there, but not the one she wanted. "Doesn't sound like a sound economic move to quit your job at a very successful firm."

Trenton spun his glass. "Funny. Isaac said the same thing. I was tired of it. I made them a lot of money. Now I just make it for myself. I've gone freelance."

Ginny sipped her wine. "This is amazing. No clients yet?"

Trenton took her glass. Spinning it, he took a sip where her lips had been. "Mmm. Very good. And just one client right now. I'm taking a long-overdue vacation of sorts."

Ginny took her glass when he handed it back to him. "You're smooth, I'll give you that."

Trenton didn't respond.

Ginny changed the subject. "How long have you known Dr. Brandt?"

Trenton cringed. "Isaac, please. Even he hates it when he's called that. He makes his students call him professor. I've known him since I was twelve. I had just moved in with my aunt and uncle. They put me in a private school. But I hated it, and my grades were terrible. That's how I met Isaac. He was my tutor."

"That's a nice story. You two have been friends for a long time. Has he always had a talent for writing?"

Trenton glanced up. The waiter set their food down and

left. "You'd have to ask him. He never showed us until he started teaching. But he was always the brains. Thanks to him, I graduated a year early. It was no fun being in school once Gideon, Nash, and Isaac graduated."

"Oh, I didn't realize all four of you went there. I just assumed…" Ginny let what she was about to say fade.

Trenton knew where she had been going with that. "Gideon was a special case. His mom was a single mom, and he has a younger sister. Nash and Gideon became friends, and Nash's parents thought Gideon was a good influence. So they paid for him to go to school with Nash."

Ginny made a mental note of that. No one just pays for a friend of their son to go to a private school, especially one so prestigious. Trenton didn't look like he was lying, but she had looked up the cost of it. The pieces didn't fit.

All she said was, "That's very generous."

Trenton pointed to her plate. "Eat up while it's hot. I have a feeling you won't stop talking to actually enjoy it. And I can guarantee you it's delicious. This is my favorite place to eat."

Ginny flushed. It had been years since she'd eaten a hot meal while out on a date. He did have her pegged there. But most of her dinners were like this one, more business than pleasure. Though she had a feeling if she were to let go and treat this like a date, she would enjoy it more than she'd be comfortable with.

Trenton took a bite. "I can see the wheels spinning in that pretty head of yours."

Ginny took a bite. It was delicious. "Occupational hazard. I'm always trying to put the puzzle pieces together.

The story gets easier as you get the rest of the picture. But you're right. This is delicious. I can see why you come here. So why not bring all your dates here?"

Trenton gave her a facetious grin. "I don't want to trip over all my old girlfriends every time I come here to eat."

Ginny laughed. "And there is the real truth. Well, I don't live around here, so you won't be tripping over me."

Trenton's gaze became serious. "I wouldn't mind."

Ginny wanted to laugh it off but couldn't. "Look, Trenton. I'm here to do research for a book. And to do an article. I'm not here to find romance."

Trenton took a sip of his water. "Sometimes you don't have a choice. I admit, I admire your work. I was excited to meet you. But as soon as I saw you, I stopped seeing Ginny Page, the writer. I saw a desirable woman. One I would like to get to know better."

Ginny's lashes lowered. When he looked at her like that, like he meant every word, she wished she were there for any other reason than why she had sought him out. But he couldn't know why she was here. And he couldn't know who she really was. Her life might just depend on it.

* * *

Trenton unlocked the front door of his home only half an hour from the restaurant where he had parted ways with Ginny. She was a puzzle. A sexy one, but still a puzzle. She had deflected any personal questions he'd thrown her way. He'd asked her where she was from, and all she said was Utah. He asked if she had siblings, and all she said was two.

From there he'd asked about boyfriends, and she flat-out refused to answer him.

Trenton unbuttoned the cuffs of his dress shirt and rolled up the sleeves. He went to his office and booted his computer up. If Ginny wasn't going to answer his questions, then he'd learn them for himself. The information he found was basic; he knew who she was and the books and articles she'd written.

There was a brief comment that she had a bachelor's degree in journalism, but not much else. He had skipped university and traveled. The quartet took the year after he'd graduated from high school to see some of the world. Gideon had already been working toward becoming a cop, so he'd only gone on a couple of trips, but Trenton had dragged Isaac and Nash with him on the majority of them. It was easy with Nash. Trenton tagged along with him wherever Nash was doing a photo shoot. Eventually he finished an accelerated degree program and got his bachelor's in business. It seemed so long ago.

But Ginny Page didn't have much else out there that he could find. The simple biography didn't tell him anything that her book jacket didn't. Two hours later, he was frustrated. He sat back in his seat. He then grabbed his cell. He dialed Gideon.

Gideon answered in his usual terse tone. "Eginhard."

Trenton smiled. "You're the only person I know who answers his phone without looking at who's calling first. And uses his last name to identify himself."

Gideon's chair creaked loudly enough that Trenton could hear it. "It's a cop thing. I'm busy. What's up?"

"Ginny Page is what's up."

Gideon grunted; a usual response. "What about her?"

"That's the question. I can't seem to find much about her."

Gideon's chair creaked again. "What do you mean?"

Trenton could tell he had Gideon's attention. Because of their history and the bonds they shared, anything out of the ordinary was followed up on. "Well, first she's a reporter. Second, we had dinner, and she evaded all my questions. Third, she seems to have popped up out of nowhere six years ago right before her first book came out. I can't find anything else."

Gideon was on full alert. "Nash."

Trenton hated to say it, but he could be right. "What if she's here to dig into Nash's history? She wouldn't be the first reporter to try to dredge up his grandfather's murder. And she wouldn't be the first who tried to find dirt on the Camhion family."

Gideon tapped a few keys loudly enough that Trenton could hear the taps. "That whole mess was covered up. There never was a hint of anything more than the murder. And it made for a juicy enough story back then that there was no reason for anyone to dig deeper. But if Ms. Page is looking for a bigger story than Isaac or Cantwell, then we need to be on alert."

Trenton gazed at his screen. "I'll call Nash. But I wonder if we should contact a private investigator to look into her past. I don't want you to get in trouble for digging into a private citizen's business."

Gideon's response was a murmur. "She doesn't have any

traffic tickets, and there are no warrants. She doesn't have a criminal history, which is good news. But given what we know of her, or don't know, I think your suggestion might be a good idea. You seem to have charmed her. You should keep an eye on her and make sure she doesn't stumble into anything she shouldn't."

Trenton's eyes danced. "That wouldn't be a hardship."

Gideon grunted again. "I had a feeling it wouldn't be. You were on your best behavior when you met her. I assume you dazzled her at dinner."

Trenton wasn't so sure, but she hadn't run out on him either. "Some. But not enough. I'll have to work harder next time."

"You think she will agree to a next time?"

Trenton didn't have to think before he spoke. "Oh, yeah."

Trenton's next call was to Nash.

Nash was ever practical. "Look. It's old news. There is no reason why anyone would care about a murder that's twenty-five years old. People have short memories."

Trenton wished he could be as sure as Nash sounded. "It's a cold case. Things get stirred up, new evidence comes to light, and then it comes out that it wasn't just a murder."

There was silence on the line. Then Nash's voice came back, this time with a hint of grief. "Gideon has been trying to find my grandfather's murderer and my kidnapper since he joined the force. Gideon has chased every lead, no matter how small or ridiculous it sounded. It pains me. You know how much it pains me. But his killer is never going to be caught. He might not even be alive anymore.

And after what happened to Penny, I just want to forget. And Gideon needs to forget, too. He has a wife now, and he needs to learn how to be happy and how to keep her happy."

Trenton doubted Nash would ever forget. And the deep gut sorrow in Nash's voice made him sorry he'd called. Nash had lived through hell at the hands of his kidnapper. When Penny had been threatened and then kidnapped four months ago, Trenton wasn't sure Nash was going to survive. Not only because of the fire that almost claimed his life, but because of the trauma that would have struck him if he'd lost his sister. And because it was their cousin Clara, whom they loved and worked with every day, who had orchestrated it, the pain went that much deeper for the family.

Nash changed the subject. "My father and Hayden are still speaking. Dad is thinking about giving Hayden a job with the company. I know my dad feels guilty, but I don't like this one bit. And now that Hayden's heart has gotten weaker, I feel like Dad is trying to make amends before he dies. I just want Hayden to disappear. And I don't want him at the office anywhere near Penny."

Trenton was shocked. "So with Clara dead, he hires Clara's dad to join the ranks? The guy who embezzled money and disappeared? I don't know what to say about that one."

Trenton imagined Nash's nonchalant shoulder shrug that he used when the tension was getting to be too much. "Dad says people deserve second chances. I say let him go back to whatever rock he crawled out from under. I don't believe for a moment he's remorseful. Penny is on the fence, but her soft streak is more than a mile wide. She'd forgive Clara if she were still alive. But with Penny at the helm of Camhion Enterprises, Hayden will no doubt try to sway and manipulate her feelings."

Trenton thought of Penny, with her blonde hair and lovely smile. "She likes to see the good in people. She sees the good in Gideon, so it's good enough for me."

Gideon and Penny had circled each other for years. Gideon had avoided Penny at all costs. But when the women in the Camhion family were threatened, Penny had sought out Gideon. Gideon had promised to protect Nash's sister. He'd kept that promise. And then he'd married her.

Nash murmured something to someone in the room, then came back on the line. "I've got to go. Lilah and I are working out some kinks in the code. Look, I'm not worried about a nosy reporter, even if she's here looking for a big story. Twenty-five years is a long time to keep a secret. The only people who know are the quartet, my parents, Penny, and the police. And unfortunately, so does Hayden. But it's not likely anyone would think to talk to him about it. None of us are going to give away our secrets."

"And the killer. He knows."

Nash's voice was full of fire. "I wish he'd show his face. After I'm done with him, he'll wish he were dead. And then I'd let Gideon have him."

Trenton wasn't convinced that the quartet wouldn't tear the man to pieces if they knew who he was. "For his sake, he had better hope Gideon never discovers who he is."

Trenton hung up and dialed the number he really wanted to call. The line rang six times before it was picked up.

"Hello, Trenton."

Trenton sat down and leaned back in his chair. "Hi, Ginny. Just checking to make sure you made it home safe. Wherever home is right now."

Ginny's voice held amusement. "I'm not going to tell you where I'm staying. But it was a good try."

Trenton picked up a pen and twirled it. "How about we spend the day together on Friday? I know you're meeting with Isaac tomorrow. But Isaac has a class on Friday, and he won't miss it. So you might as well say yes."

Trenton could picture Ginny pacing her hotel room, trying to decide if she should say yes. "Where would we go?"

Trenton glanced at the photo of the four men on his bookcase. "How about I take you out on my boat? The day is expected to be beautiful. I'll pack lunch, and we can cruise. And I'll tell you whatever you want to know about Cantwell."

"And?"

He could picture the wheels spinning in her mind. "And anything else you might want to know. How about that?"

"How can a girl refuse?"

That's what he was counting on.

* * *

Ginny debated all morning about what to wear. She asked Trenton where he'd like her to meet him. He'd said his house. So she was going to drive over there, and he was going to drive them out to the marina. She had started to protest when he said his house, but she'd relented when he said it was a private club, and she'd need him to get her in. She could have simply met him there, but admittedly she was curious about his home. She'd seen pictures of it on the web, both on Google Maps and on society sites, but she wanted to see it firsthand.

He wasn't what she'd expected. Well, she supposed she wasn't sure what she had expected. Somewhere between shrewd and charismatic. Like his father. But there was a casualness about him. He teased his friends, he flirted with her, and he'd done his best to charm her at dinner. She hated to admit it, but he had succeeded. For a moment, she had forgotten why she had sought him out. She had forgotten that he could be dangerous to her and her family.

And at the end of the night, there had been no pushing him away, or trying to stave off wandering hands and lips. He'd played the gentleman, walking her to her car, and then calling her to see if she'd like to see him again. He knew the answer would be yes. They both knew it. If Cantwell were the only reason she was here, she might have run. Men hit on her. Men flirted with her. Men tried to use her for both personal and financial gain. But Trenton hadn't given off any of the vibes that would have sent her alarms ringing.

"Gentiana, get with it." Ginny only used her first name when she was frustrated with herself. Sometimes it was like someone else lived inside her, and it took work to suppress her. Two people, two lives, two personalities. Gentiana was the young, scared girl she'd been. Gentiana was the young wife who didn't know how to cope with an unwanted and sometimes abusive husband. Ginny was strong. Ginny was in control. But Ginny, the adult, was scared, too. And Ginny was also a mother, and scared or not, she'd protect her daughter.

Ginny took a few moments to center herself and finished getting ready. She dusted on light makeup, pulled her hair back so her sun hat would fit over her hair, and opted to wear loose-fitting beige linen pants paired with a lightweight cotton shirt. She hoped Trenton had opted for casual clothes, versus the suits she'd seen him in the two times they'd met.

The drive across town allowed her to practice deep breathing and relax. The neighborhood was quiet, and the small mansions that lined the streets were impressive. Ginny preferred apartments; no commitments. But oh, how she did wish she could raise her daughter in a beautiful home like these ones, with a strong, loving, caring man waiting for her. One that would love and cherish his family.

That is the one, Ginny thought. She didn't even have to look at the house number to know this one was where Trenton lived. The champagne brick and terracotta tile roof seemed his style. There was a large willow tree in the middle of the front lawn, and a brick pathway wound around it to the front door.

She grabbed her shoulder bag and locked her rental car door behind her. She had only made it halfway across the walkway before the door opened. Her steps faltered for a second.

"I was wondering if you would show." Trenton waved her in.

Ginny swallowed and followed him inside. The interior was light and modern. The entryway floors were beautiful, oversized tile. She didn't know décor, but she liked what she saw.

Trenton closed the door behind him. "Come on in. I can give you the tour if you'd like."

Ginny gave him her best smile. "I'd love one."

Trenton took her bag and set it on the side table. "What is in this thing?"

Ginny let Trenton take her arm. "Life's essentials."

Trenton laughed. "You sound like Penny."

Ginny memorized the layout of the house as he walked her through it. He was very knowledgeable about the antique furniture he collected. The mix of antique and modern should have clashed, but somehow, he made it mesh.

"You look bored." Trenton took her to the kitchen.

Ginny accepted the bottle of sparkling water Trenton handed her. "Not bored. But I don't know much about antiques. Most of my furniture is rented."

Trenton shuddered. "I can't even imagine having rented furniture. Let me guess, it's all beige and gray?"

Ginny shrugged and took a sip of her water. "Mostly. But I move around a lot, so it's just easier not to have to deal with movers. As long as I have my laptop and my tablet, I can set up anywhere."

Trenton bit his lip. "Anywhere, huh? I've got a spare room."

"Not quite as smooth as at dinner. But my hotel has a tiny desk and a view of the parking lot. Makes me feel at home."

Trenton took her arm again. "Your idea of home and mine varies significantly. I'll show you upstairs."

Ginny counted five bedrooms and three bathrooms. As she stood in the doorway of the master, admiring the soft blue and gray tones, she felt a moment of envy. "It's a lot of house. And a beautiful one."

Trenton stepped in front of her and gazed down at her soft expression. "That might be the first honest thing you've said to me since we met."

Ginny heard her wistful tone and cursed herself. "It's, of course, not my style."

Trenton took her wrist. "Yes, your taste runs to cheap hotel décor."

Ginny looked at his hand holding her. "At least I don't have to clean it. Can I have my arm back?"

Trenton dropped her arm. "You have no idea how badly I want to kiss you right now."

Ginny had noticed. And she wanted him to. "Just one."

Trenton's eyes opened wide in surprise. But he didn't question her. He tipped her chin with one knuckle and brought his mouth to hers.

Ginny wasn't sure what possessed her to say that. But kissing him felt inevitable. And when he pressed his lips to hers, all thought of just one kiss fled. Her hands went to his shoulders for balance, and she found herself kissing him back. He dropped his hands to her waist, as if using her to keep both of them upright. She felt dizzy from the kiss. She wasn't sure she was breathing. She wanted to deepen the kiss, to taste all of him, but self-preservation stopped her.

She pulled back and took a gulp of air, holding him until her legs were steady.

Trenton did much of the same. Once his breathing slowed, he spoke. "We need to get out of here. I promised you a boat ride."

Ginny took a step back. "So you did."

Ginny followed him downstairs to the kitchen. He pulled a tote out of the oversized fridge.

Trenton then grabbed a cooler he had tucked by the door. "Grab the bag, and I'll grab the cooler. We'll take my car."

Ginny took the bag from him and followed him through the side door. The three-car garage only had one car in it. She had gotten a glimpse of it at the restaurant. The bright red Porsche was hard to miss. "Nice car."

Trenton popped the trunk and stowed the bag and cooler. He didn't reply to her comment. "Top up or down?"

Ginny pulled the hat from her bag. "Down."

Trenton nodded in approval.

Ginny enjoyed the drive to the marina. He handled the sports car effortlessly. She'd never been in one before, and she was suitably impressed. "I'm guessing you do take your dates out in this, unlike your favorite restaurant."

Trenton smiled, his mirrored sunglasses hiding his eyes. "Chicks dig it."

Ginny figured she had asked for that. So she simply sat back and enjoyed the fresh air as he drove the winding roads. The ride took an hour, but both of them were content with light conversation or silence.

Ginny also didn't spend much time near water. She liked

the beach well enough, but she'd never been on a boat. And "boat" was a gross understatement. The yacht was all sleek lines, much like his car. He carried the food and the cooler aboard while she gaped. He went through a door before emerging to help her aboard.

"I've never seen anything like this. I thought you meant like a sailboat or something."

Trenton took her hand and showed her around, much like he had his home. "The kitchen and bar are covered with a canopy that can be opened to let the sun in. Below deck, I have a master bedroom and bath, and a guest bed and bath. There is also a living room with two oversized couches built into the walls. Then there is another smaller kitchen inside for when it's cold or raining."

Whites and blues covered most of the surfaces. She heard him telling her specs and something about the motor, but she wasn't listening anymore. This was money like she'd never seen. The house. The car. The boat. Anxiety filled her belly. When she sought him out, she didn't know what to expect. But seeing all this, what all this represented, frightened her more than she wanted to admit.

Trenton led her to the sofa. "You look ill. Do you get seasick?"

Ginny sat down hard. "I don't know."

Trenton sat down beside her and took her wrist. He pressed the pulse point. "Let's just sit here for a minute. If your heart rate doesn't come down, we can have our picnic on land."

Ginny took several deep breaths. She'd rather have him think she was seasick than afraid. It took a few minutes to relax.

"There you go." Trenton released her. "Let's go above board. We can eat docked. How does that sound?"

Ginny nodded and let him steady her as she climbed the stairs. "I'm sorry. It's a beautiful boat."

Trenton went about fixing lunch. "No need to be sorry. This is my favorite spot. And honestly, I love traveling this way. I've been meaning to take a trip for a few weeks, but with the wedding and Cantwell full steam ahead, the timing isn't right."

Ginny had read the newspapers and watched the news when she had been researching Trenton. "And I guess with everything that went on before. I read about what happened to the Camhion family. Your friend Penny and what happened with her cousin. It's terrifying when you can't trust your own family."

Trenton turned and set down the plate he had fixed. "And what of it?"

Ginny shivered at the tone and the look in his eyes. She stammered. "Nothing. I just read about it. Must have been terrifying."

Trenton's body relaxed. "It was. And yes, being that it was her cousin made dealing with the aftermath worse. I take it you don't have a great relationship with your family. You said it's terrifying when you can't trust your family."

Ginny realized what she had said and silently cursed herself. Again, she opted for mostly truth. "I didn't have a great relationship with my dad. He was a scary man. My mom tried to leave him a few times, but she kept going back. When she died, that was the last time I saw him."

Trenton went back to fixing their meal. "I'm sorry about your mom. I don't remember my parents much. Both died when I was young. My aunt and uncle took me in. They're great. But I remember being so scared when they came and got me."

Ginny was quiet for a few minutes. "You said you'd answer any of my questions if I came."

Trenton served the rest of the meal and took a seat across from her. "So I did. I'm thirty-six, single, live alone, love boats and cars, and have the best friends a man could have. I recently quit my job to freelance. My life is an open book. Your turn."

Ginny couldn't help but laugh. "That is probably the shortest summary of someone's life I've heard in my career. Most people love to talk about themselves."

"I'm not most people."

Ginny silently agreed. "Okay, so I'm thirty-two, single, travel for work, and I can't say I have a ton of friends. Family, either. I guess as a writer, you could say I freelance. My agent and my publisher love me and let me write pretty much whatever I want."

Trenton shook his head. "What does Ginny stand for? Jennifer? Virginia?"

Ginny bit the side of her lip. She supposed it didn't hurt to answer him. "No. Gentiana."

"Wow. I would never have guessed that. That is very unique. Family name?"

Ginny slowly shook her head. "No. My mom chose it for me. She said I was her beautiful flower. Gentiana is a genus of flowers that is often a vibrant blue. She said it was the color of my eyes when I was born."

"And a beautiful blue it is."

Ginny dropped her gaze so that her lashes hid her eyes. "Anyway, Ginny is easier to say and spell for a little girl. It stuck with me as a kid, and professionally it made sense to keep it."

Both were silent for a while as they ate. Ginny was at a loss for words. She was drawn to Trenton, and it was the last thing she expected. He was charming, no doubt. He had a sense of humor, though it was tamed today. Enigma was the word she was looking for. Nothing about him added up. Nothing of what she saw of him made sense to her. She thought she would meet him, see through his lies, and expose him for who she knew him to be. But when she looked at him and listened to him, she didn't see or hear lies.

Chapter Four

"You seem very pensive, Ginny. Thinking about the kiss?"

Ah, the kiss. That, too, she wasn't sure how to explain. But it was as good a reason as any. "I don't get involved with the subjects of my work. Professionally speaking, it was very unprofessional of me to kiss you."

Trenton leaned back in his seat. "I won't tell anyone. So how about we finish your work, so we don't have to worry about professionalism anymore? You write your article, and then I won't be the subject of your work."

Ginny mirrored his pose. "That's very practical of you. And you're half right. I do have an article to write. So tell me about Cantwell. I read the book, and I can imagine it in game form."

"Lilah can show you some of what we've done. But Nash is the reason we created Cantwell. Nash is, shall we say, a bit disillusioned with life. It sounds trite, but there is a bit of the poor rich kid syndrome in his life. I assume you researched all of us."

Ginny didn't play coy. "I know his grandfather was murdered when he was thirteen. I found the story almost immediately when I searched Camhions of D.C. That had to be traumatic. The reports say he witnessed it, and a bystander whisked him out of the way before he was hurt or shot. I imagine the damage had already been done the moment he saw his grandfather shot. I also saw some very flattering pictures of him when he modeled. Your friend is quite the ladies' man."

"He is. I've seen women literally swoon at his feet. And he's basically a nice guy. Just hasn't found the right woman yet."

Ginny took her tablet out of her bag. "I could say the same about you. You seem like basically a nice guy. I'm not exactly swooning at your feet, though I would say you're attractive. So instead of staying with the family business after he modeled, he turned it over to his sister Penelope and went the playboy route for a while before forming Cantwell."

"Penny is the one who takes after their father and grandfather. Nash has tinkered with a few different things over the years when he gets bored playing the socialite. To appease his father, he has a law degree. But he has been toying with the idea of a game for a while. One afternoon he was hanging out with Isaac and read his rough draft. Nash fell in love with the story and immediately called all of us up to meet. Isaac polished the draft and handed it over to Gideon and me, and frankly, we were blown away by it. Gideon started doodling, and I kept thinking about all the photographs I've taken and what would fit the story."

Ginny held up a hand. "Stop. You said you were the money. What photos?"

Trenton pointed to the door into the living area. "The framed photos on the walls are ones I took. The good ones, anyway. I do photography as a hobby when I'm on vacation. I can't tell you how many thousands of photos I have taken. I knew there were some I'd taken that would fit the scenery of the story. So I keep track of the money, but I also help put storyboards together. Mostly scenery."

Ginny set her tablet down and went into the living room. She went to the larger of the framed photographs. It was a landscape taken on the top of a cliff, overlooking a forest area. The black-and-white print caught the sunlight as it peeked over the cliff and poured over the trees. "You took this?"

Trenton stayed in his seat but could see what she was looking at. "I did. Ireland is my favorite place to go. Most of the photos I used are from there. Other photos I used are from New Zealand. Another favorite place to visit. There's a reason so many movies are filmed in New Zealand. It's a small world unto itself. But Ireland has this mystical feel to it, as if you would see the fairies and leprechauns of legend in the mists."

Ginny took in the rest of the photos. "All of these are yours, aren't they?"

"Yeah."

Ginny came and stood in the doorway. "I would say you're the money and the artist. Those are beautiful."

Trenton waved for her to come sit and finish her meal. "Lilah keeps trying to get me to show them to a gallery. I'm not interested."

Ginny thought of the tall redhead. Fitzpatrick, red hair, fair skin, and freckles. Definitely Irish. And attractive. "How does Lilah fit in?"

Trenton took Ginny's hand. He rubbed his fingers over

her knuckles. "Lilah has become a friend. But Nash found her. Nash is good with computers, and one of his hobbies is coding and design. But he's not an expert. He knew he'd need help. A friend of his told him about Lilah. She'd just been fired from her job. I'll let her tell you why if she wants to. But don't bet on it. Nash called her and talked to her about potentially working for us. He liked what he saw immediately. It was another couple of months before he reached out again and gave her the job. She quit her new job that day and came to work for Cantwell."

Ginny's gaze dropped to their linked hands. "She seemed nice. It does seem odd that Nash didn't hire a man, given that there are four males who own the company."

Trenton's left brow rose. "I think that might be sexist. Lilah is perfect. And she doesn't bring a fifth male ego into the mix. The four of us agreed to hire her based on what Nash said, not her gender."

Ginny flushed. "I suppose that did sound sexist. And I get a fifth male ego. You're an eclectic bunch. She seems to fit in. I've not had the chance to meet with her, Gideon, or Nash for a one-on-one yet. It will be interesting to see what they have to say. Isaac was flattering, but it was probably not his intent. He's a very serious man."

Trenton kept rubbing her fingers. "Usually. I like to think I help lighten him up. But academically speaking, the guy is a genius. He likes Georgetown, but he could have taken a job at any university. There have been many over the years who have offered him prestigious positions. He says he has no plans to leave. But being around other historians, students, and English literature students all the time, he tends to fall into lecture mode. Drives Lilah crazy."

"And yet his books are the opposite." Ginny extracted her fingers. Even that small touch was making her insides quiver.

Trenton looked pleased when she pulled away. "What else, Ms. Page?"

She didn't want to ask any more questions. Some of the fear she felt earlier came back. She wanted him to be exactly what he appeared to be: a wealthy, funny, charming, smooth-talking, attractive male.

Trenton must have seen the combination of fear and desire that was swirling inside her. He rose and came around the table. He looked down at her and held out his hand.

Ginny laid her hand in his, and he pulled her into his arms. She wrapped her arms around his neck when his hands wove into her hair. She felt her breasts swell against his chest. He simply held her, waiting for her to make the next move. Wanting to curse herself for her weakness when it came to this man, she stood on her toes and brought her mouth to his. This time she kissed him as she had wanted to before. She opened her mouth when his tongue probed her lips. Not breaking contact with her mouth, Trenton lifted her into his arms and took her to one of the long sofas in his living room. She felt her back hit the cushions and Trenton's weight come down on top of her. She heard the whimper that escaped her, not recognizing the sound as having come from her.

Trenton's knee slid between her legs as he settled more of his weight on her. His hands once again threaded through her hair. His mouth left hers and trailed wet kisses to her throat. She heard that disassociated whimper again. She tipped her head so he had better access. She grabbed the hem of his shirt and trailed her fingers up his bare back. She barely registered the muscles there when his mouth found hers once more.

Trenton released her hair, bracing one hand next to her as his other found the hem of her shirt while he kissed her. His fingers teased the skin of her stomach as his hand trailed to her breast. He found the underside of her breast and eased his hand under her bra so he could cup the flesh he found. Her breasts weren't large, but when his fingers plucked her nipple, she felt her breast swell under those experienced fingers.

Trenton's other knee found its way between her thighs. When his erection pressed against her through her thin linen pants and underwear, she froze. What was she doing?

Her sudden tension was palpable. Trenton stopped. "Ginny?"

Ginny's eyes flew to his. She tried to speak, but she couldn't find her voice. But she knew the moment he saw what she was trying to say.

Trenton eased onto his knees and maneuvered away from her until he was sitting on the couch. He took her arms and pulled her up and over so that she was sitting next to him. He gently tugged her against his side and held her when she didn't pull away.

Ginny could hear his rough breathing as her forehead lay against his chest and knew he, too, was trying to calm himself, though for a different reason.

It was a few minutes before he spoke. "Want to talk about it?"

Ginny eased away. "No."

"Want to leave?"

Ginny sighed. "No."

Trenton kept his eyes off her. "Do me a favor, then?"

"What?"

"Fix your bra."

Ginny looked down and her nipples were clearly beaded against the fabric. Blushing, she fixed it through her top.

Trenton rose. "I'm going to clean up our meal. Want to try to go out on the water? The water doesn't get much calmer than it is today."

"How about I clean up the mess, and you get the boat ready?"

Trenton finally looked at her. He smiled softly at her. "It's a deal. You'll have to wash and put them away. Once the boat is moving, we can't have anything loose."

They separated once on the deck. Ginny put the rest of the food into the outside fridge. She then washed and dried the dishes. It was nice to clean up while watching the boats around her rock on the water. It took her a few minutes to put everything away, and by the time she was done, Trenton called for her to join him.

She took a seat where he pointed and watched as he expertly turned on the engine and guided them out of the marina. She could see the muscles in his arms flex as he steered. His mirrored glasses were once again in place, so she couldn't see his eyes, though she could feel them when they drifted her way. Once away from the rest of the boats, he increased the speed and took them out into open water.

She supposed she should have had him take her back to her car. She never intended what had happened between them. There was something incredibly magnetic about him. She hadn't been afraid of him. She had enjoyed kissing him, enjoyed the weight of him on her body. His skin had been smooth, and his muscles sleek under her palms. At that moment, she had wanted him. Had wanted sex with him. A desire she had never experienced had taken over. But the fear and panic she was familiar with when she'd felt his erection had abruptly taken control and she'd froze. She knew she owed him an explanation, even if it weren't the truth. But deep down she hesitated to tell any more lies. But she couldn't tell him the truth. She just couldn't face it yet.

* * *

Trenton could feel Ginny's tension all the way over where he stood. She was biting her lip, and her eyes were cloudy. He could see her trying to work through her thoughts. He could also see she hadn't come to a conclusion yet.

Fear. He didn't think it had been aimed at him, but it had been tangible. He'd seen that fear before. Not directed at him, but in his mother's eyes every time his father came. So he'd pulled away from her, but he hadn't wanted to walk away. Now on the water, he was glad she had opted to stay. She might not be ready today, but he wasn't going to give up on her.

A mile out, where they could still see the shore, he cut the engine and let the boat drift. Trenton walked over to the side and watched the water. He smiled at Ginny when she came to stand next to him.

Ginny gripped the railing. "This is nice. I can see why you enjoy this. Might be hard to sleep with all the movement, though."

Trenton kept his knee-jerk comment to himself about movement and rocking. "You get used to it. When I come home after being out on the water for a while, I find it hard to sleep without it."

Ginny kept her eyes forward. "Aren't you going to ask me again?"

Trenton leaned his forearms on the railing and watched the water. "No."

Ginny huffed. "Most men would be really mad right now. Would call me a tease."

Trenton straightened and pulled his sunglasses off. "You're not a tease. You were scared. That was not the mood I was going for. And in a way, you're right. It's too soon."

Ginny crossed her arms over her chest. "I didn't know there was a 'too soon' when it comes to men."

"For me, it depends on the woman. But despite what you read in the society pages, I don't date that many women. And I do like to know a woman better before I take her to bed. I guess part of me feels like I already know you."

"My books." Ginny rubbed the chill from her arms.

Trenton closed his eyes as he tipped his head to the sun. "Yes. I admire your work. Having met you, I admire you more. You have a quick mind. And when you're not giving me your fake smile, I enjoy your company."

Ginny frowned at him. "My fake smile?"

Trenton nodded. "The one you gave me the day we met."

"Ah, my 'you can trust me' smile. It's my reporter smile. You're the first one to call me out on it." She shivered.

Trenton glanced at Ginny. "Cold?"

"No. Confused."

Trenton agreed. "Same. How about we make a deal? Don't ever give me that fake smile again, and I won't ask you what scared you. How about that?"

Ginny glanced at him and gave him a genuine smile. "Deal. I have a question for you."

Trenton laughed. "Don't you have several?"

Ginny responded to his laughter. "I suppose I do. But not right now. I'm having a nice afternoon. You didn't date Lilah, did you?"

Trenton's brow rose at that. "No. I told you, we're friends. Besides, Isaac is in love with her. He'll deny it, of course."

"You two seem sort of an obvious couple. You love Ireland and all. And she's really cute; she could be on a travel poster for Ireland."

Trenton slipped his arm around Ginny's shoulders. "That she could. But I'm starting to like brunettes."

Ginny relaxed against him, and they watched the water and the shore in the distance.

* * *

It was almost dark when Trenton docked the boat. Ginny had relaxed, and they enjoyed the rest of the afternoon. He wasn't sure he should have made the deal not to ask what happened to her, but it had been what she needed to pull out of her thoughts. He could see she was still trying to figure out how much she should tell him. For all intents and purposes, they were still strangers.

"That was really nice, Trenton. I'd love to do that again."

Trenton took her hand as they walked back to the parking lot. "I'm glad you liked it. Spend any amount of time with me, and you'll definitely end up back on the boat."

Ginny squeezed his hand. "You are the master of understatements. You own a mansion you call a house. You own a yacht you call a boat. And a Porsche you call a car."

Trenton pulled her to a stop. "It's because that's what they are. They're nice, don't get me wrong. But they are not what makes me who I am. I don't define myself by things. So when people tell you they own a mansion, or a yacht, or a Porsche, it's because that's how they define themselves. I could lose all my money on one bad investment, Ginny. I like money. I like not having to worry about how I'm going to survive day to day. I enjoy the things it can buy. But I'll never let money or things define me."

Ginny looked into his eyes. "You really mean that."

Trenton was relieved when she resumed walking, and he followed.

His curse broke their silence. He pulled her behind him as he increased their pace. Shattered glass lay on the ground around his car. "Son of a…"

Ginny stepped carefully around the glass. "Your car."

"Don't touch anything. I'll call the cops."

Ginny rooted where she stood. Trenton tried to pull her back, but she didn't budge. Her eyes were fixed on the inside of his car.

Trenton looked where she was. On the passenger seat lay a book. One of Ginny's books. The word "liar" was written in red on the cover. He cursed again and reached for his phone.

Ginny grabbed his wrist. "Please, don't. Don't call the police."

Trenton's eyes narrowed. "Ginny, someone broke into my car. And that looks like a threat to me. I'm calling the cops."

Ginny grabbed his shirt, trying to make him understand. "Don't. If you call them, you'll learn the truth."

Trenton's hands lay on top of hers. "What truth?"

"That I am a liar."

Chapter Five

Ginny let go of Trenton's shirt as she tried to stem her tears. "Please, Trenton. Please don't call them. I'll pay for the damage."

"Why?"

"I can't tell you why. Not yet."

Trenton hesitated. "Do you know who did this?"

Ginny wiped her eyes, the tears still falling. "Yes. I don't know his name, but I know who did it. You have to trust me."

Trenton wasn't convinced. He pulled out his phone. "Gideon, I need some help. Someone smashed my car window and left a threat. Ginny is with me. I'd like you to come. Alone."

Ginny could barely hear Gideon on the phone, but she was pretty sure he was swearing. Trenton told him where they were and hung up.

"It's going to take him a while to get here. You need to explain this to me."

Ginny knew she had two choices. She could trust her gut and tell him the truth. Or she could exercise the same caution she'd been using the last six years.

Trenton grabbed her arm, not as gently as he had before, and moved her away from the car and toward the back of the car lot. "All right, Ginny. You either tell me, or I will have Gideon call reinforcements. No more games. I knew something was wrong the day we met. This is about Nash, isn't it?"

Ginny watched as he started pacing. Her confusion was genuine. "Nash?"

Trenton turned on her. "Murder. It makes for a great story. I knew I had better keep an eye on you. I knew not to trust you. You're either here because of Cormac Camhion's murder, or to dig up dirt on Nash or the family. It's the only thing that makes sense. I knew it."

Her voice was a whisper when she spoke. "Keeping an eye on me? Is that what you've been doing?"

Trenton spun on his heel and paced in the other direction. "Damn straight."

Ginny knew she didn't deserve to feel hurt. She had done nothing but lie to him since she arrived. Or, she supposed, withheld the truth. She doubted he would see the difference. She knew she didn't. But it did hurt that the only reason he wanted to see her was to keep an eye on her.

Ginny sat on the curb and watched him pace.

Trenton stopped and looked down at her. "The truth, Ginny."

Ginny folded her arms on her lap. "I'm not here because of Nash. Or because of the Camhion family. I'm here because of you."

Trenton scoffed. "Why not Isaac? Or Gideon? There is no reason you would be here because of me."

Ginny looked him in the eye. "I know who you are."

That stopped Trenton cold. "What do you mean?"

Ginny tried to figure out the best place to start. Maybe it

was the beginning. "Eighty years ago, a man named Hezekiah Stafford started a cult. He didn't call it that, of course. He had this idea he could make perfect people. Not unlike Hitler, he had an idea he could manipulate genetics. He did it under the guise of religion, as most cult leaders do. He sought out younger people whom he could recruit; people he thought were perfect specimens for his experiments. Using religion, he gained a following. He'd cull out those he found desirable and segregate them. The rest he used for various purposes. They grew their own food, made their own clothes, and lived off the grid, using today's lingo."

Trenton swallowed. Hard. "What do you know of it?"

Ginny continued. "He had a son. Two of them. But his first son was his favorite. He named him Jeremiah. The boy was raised by his father; his mother was kept from him. Jeremiah became the perfect son, eventually taking over the cult when Hezekiah became too old. Jeremiah took his father's place and continued on after his death. There was one woman Jeremiah wanted to be the mother of his first son, a woman named Sarah, who had been born into the cult. Some people say Sarah dreamed of leaving. Said she was horrified when Jeremiah had chosen her to bear his first son. But bear a son she did. Jeremiah named him Elijah."

Trenton took a step forward and glared at her, but didn't stop her.

Ginny swallowed and continued. "Sarah was eventually tossed aside, and Jeremiah took over raising Elijah. Jeremiah tried with many other women to have more sons, but the children were all girls. He tossed them aside, too. But one day, when the boy was eleven, Sarah worked up the courage to take Elijah. She and a few others who wanted to escape made a plan. Jeremiah caught Sarah and beat her so badly that she died from her injuries. But her lover, a man named Adam, took revenge and killed Jeremiah. Adam and a few others managed to escape, taking Elijah and a few other children with them."

Trenton's hand trembled. He picked up the story. "Sarah knew who her grandmother was. Her mother had pictures of her family before she joined the cult, even though it was forbidden. Sarah's mother was a devotee and had married the man chosen for her. The two only had one child, which they named Sarah from the bible. Sarah found the pictures her mother had kept when her mother died. Sarah told Adam who the woman was and her name. Sarah's grandmother had passed by the time the cult members escaped. With the help of the police, Elijah was taken in by his great-aunt, Sarah's grandmother's younger sister. Her name was Emily. Emily and her husband changed Elijah's name and told everyone they had adopted him. Which was the truth. They were a childless older couple, so no one questioned the adoption or their reason for it."

Ginny nodded. "Because of Adam, Jeremiah was dead, and the heir missing. The police raided the town where the cult lived based on both Elijah's and Adam's testimony. Some men were arrested when it was found that many of the wives were underage. The rest of the members scattered."

Trenton's skin was pale, and he looked like he might get sick. "You were one of the children who escaped, weren't you?"

Ginny felt new tears fall. "I wish I were. But no."

"Then how do you know all this? No one knows this about me."

Ginny smiled through her tears, her tone envious. "I bet your friends know. I'm glad you had confidants and people to help you growing up. I imagine you and Nash bonded."

Trenton put his fist to his stomach. "Then how do you know?"

Ginny saw headlights pull up. "I figure there's only one way you'll believe me."

Trenton watched as she lifted her blouse above her heart. A circular scar, years faded, caught the light.

* * *

Trenton stared in shock. "You have a brand."

Ginny dropped her shirt and looked over at Gideon as he made his way over. "Please, Trenton. Don't tell him. Not yet. There is more you don't know."

Trenton didn't know what to think. "Why didn't you say so when we met?"

Ginny whispered. "I thought you were him."

"Him?"

Ginny nodded. "The man whose name I don't know."

Trenton cursed. He took Ginny's hand and walked her back to the car.

Gideon looked at the couple. He had seen enough. "I

think you have a lot of explaining to do, Ms. Page."

Ginny shook her head.

Trenton didn't know what to think. Or how much to explain to Gideon. The story she told was true. He knew it. He had been there. But the brand on her chest frightened him. So he looked Gideon in the eyes as he told him. "She knows about the cult. She's part of it."

Ginny trembled. "Was. I'm not anymore. I ran six years ago. I've been trying to find the other members for the last five. Find them and expose them."

Gideon's eyes lasered in on Ginny. "And we're supposed to believe that? If I had a reason to arrest you, Ms. Page, you'd be in cuffs."

Trenton looked at Gideon. "We should bag the book. And we should have the car dusted for prints. Ginny can't have smashed the car window or left the book because she was with me on the boat. But that doesn't mean she's not part of who did."

Ginny's mouth opened and then snapped shut.

Trenton continued. "I'm not going to file a police report or file this with the insurance. But I think we need to regroup and figure out what the hell is going on."

Gideon seconded that. "I know some people who aren't cops who can help. Let me make some phone calls. It's getting late. Nash and Isaac are working tonight, so I'd rather wait until tomorrow. Penny is worried about you. She heard you on the phone. It's going to be nearly impossible to keep her out of this."

Trenton rubbed his palms over his face. "It's okay. She knows some of it. Not all, but some. I don't want her involved, but with the two of you married, that won't be possible. And I should probably call my Aunt Emily."

Trenton looked at Ginny. He wasn't sure what to do about her.

Gideon knew what he was thinking. "I'd say we take her with us, but kidnapping is illegal. It's still tempting."

Ginny shivered. "I'm not going anywhere. I came here to get answers. I'm going to get them."

Gideon got the kit he kept in his car and collected the book. He then dusted and lifted some fingerprints. "I'll need both of your prints to rule them out. I've got a tow truck coming to take the car over to a lab of a friend who can do a more thorough job."

Trenton wanted to laugh as Gideon took his and Ginny's fingerprints. "Want hair samples too?"

Gideon's lips twitched. "I'll let the forensic experts ask. Probably."

Trenton and Gideon chatted, but he was very aware of Ginny sitting nearby. She'd left them to go back to her seat on the curb.

Gideon jerked his head at Ginny. "How much does she know?"

Trenton rubbed the spot over his heart. "Too much. She knows the entire history of the cult, all the way back to Hezekiah Stafford. She knew about my dad and the fact that there were other children. I never met any of my sisters. They weren't important to him. I was the important one. I doubt the girls knew Jeremiah was their father. Once a woman gave him a daughter, he gave the woman to someone else, along with the child to raise as theirs.

Gideon, she sounded like she was there. She would have been seven."

Gideon hesitated. "Do you think she could be your sister?"

Trenton swore. That hadn't occurred to him. "I really hope not. I think we can add DNA tests to that list."

Gideon, who was as close as a brother, realized what he meant. He swore. "Hell, man, tell me it didn't get that far."

Trenton swallowed the bile that threatened to come up. "Not that far, but too far for comfort."

Gideon kept himself between Trenton and Ginny. "I don't know what we should do with her. I would hope she wouldn't sleep with her brother."

Trenton leaned over and took some deep breaths. "She stopped it. She looked afraid. She wouldn't say why. God, what if she is?"

Gideon put his arm around him to steady him. "DNA test for sure. But I was thinking more immediate. What if she skips?"

Trenton stood back up. He didn't think he was going to throw up anymore. "It was like she was reading one of her books. But this one was my biography. But she was part of the inner circle, or someone she is related to was. She has a brand."

Gideon's eyes shot to Ginny. "Oh, man. This just keeps getting worse."

Trenton glanced around Gideon. "I really thought this was about Nash."

"We both did."

The tow truck arrived and hauled off Trenton's car.

Trenton spoke briefly with Gideon and then went to get Ginny. "Gideon will take you to my house to get your car."

Ginny rose. "Aren't you afraid I'll run?"

Trenton started walking off, making her follow behind. "It's not like we can tie you up. And as Gideon said, he can't arrest you. So you go free."

When Ginny stopped, Trenton looked back at her. "What?"

Ginny opened her mouth, then shut it. "Nothing. It's late. We should go."

The ride back to Trenton's house was quiet. Gideon stayed in the car but didn't leave.

Ginny took out her keys. "I am sorry, Trenton, if it matters."

Trenton just kept his eyes on her. "Tomorrow. Nash's house. Ten. We'll see if you have the guts to show."

Ginny climbed into her car and didn't say another word. She backed out of the driveway and left.

Trenton waved Gideon off and went inside. Of all the things that Ginny Page could turn out to be, a fellow cult member was so far off the list. He went to the kitchen and poured himself a glass of Scotch.

He hated thinking about that night. He had seen his mother's beaten body. He had seen the hole in his father's chest. He'd been questioned at the police station, and one of the police officers had carelessly left the file on the desk where eleven-year-old Elijah could get a hold of it. He'd seen what had happened to both his parents. Adam's picture had been in the file because the police had booked him for murder after he had confessed what he'd done.

When they had gotten away from the rest of the escaped cult members, Adam had taken him to the police station. He'd told the cops what had happened. Trenton was never quite sure why he did it. He could simply have dumped him at the station. Maybe Adam had loved his mother, and he had done it for her. He liked to think so.

Adam had been released from police custody after his friends posted his bail. The man then disappeared with the rest of the cult members. Years later, Adam's body turned up, and Gideon told him about the man's death. Gideon, the protector of the bunch, had kept his eye out for any evidence that could be linked to the cult. Too bad Gentiana Page wasn't on that list.

Trenton poured himself another drink and swallowed it. Nightmares would come, he knew. But he needed to try to sleep. So he put the bottle back in the cupboard and went to bed.

* * *

Three hours later, across town, Ginny had given up on sleep. As soon as she got back to the hotel, she called Gwenny and checked in. She hadn't told Levi what had happened between her and Trenton. Or rather what she had told Trenton. Levi wouldn't have listened to her anyway. Levi tended to live in his own world and blanked out a lot of the life he had lived. But she trusted him with Gwenny, and that was all that mattered to her.

Instead of feigning sleep, she'd gotten dressed and gone to the bar across the street. She took a sip of her gin and tonic and shuddered. She wasn't normally a drinker but hoped the drink would help calm her down. Seeing her book on the seat of Trenton's car and the word "liar" written across it frightened her more than she wanted to admit.

She should run. She had thought Trenton could be behind the threats made to Gwenny, but she didn't believe that now. She hadn't believed it since the night they'd gone to dinner. She never would have gone to the boat alone with him if she had. And if he had been the one threatening her, she'd be dead by now. If there were any doubts, they were gone.

Sitting in the corner of the bar, she pulled her laptop out and pulled up her book. She was writing a book. That much was true. She supposed any future book on Isaac or Cantwell was now scrapped. But she was going to expose the cult and anyone she could find that was still involved. She had started a genealogy of everyone she knew, and who she had found so far. Some were willing to talk to her. Most were not.

She pulled up Trenton's lineage. She had his parents, Sarah and Jeramiah. She had managed to find a couple of his sisters, though there were more she had not found yet. But the name she focused on was his uncle, Jeremiah's brother, Joshua.

She had only told Trenton his part of the story. She hadn't told him hers. She knew by showing him the brand that she'd opened herself up to more questions than she wanted to answer. And with the cop Gideon around, she had no intention of divulging her secrets. But showing

Trenton the brand was the only way she could think of to get him to believe she was telling the truth. She had come to find him.

An hour later, Ginny packed her laptop back in her bag and took one last swallow of her drink. She left a tip on the table and headed out. The parking lot was still full; no doubt the party had just started for some. She crossed the street and headed towards the hotel. One bored employee wearing earbuds behind the counter was the only person in the lobby. She came around the corner, digging her keycard out of her bag.

A hand shot out of nowhere, clamping over her mouth in a vice grip. A second arm came around her waist. She thrashed, trying to get loose, but the man kept his grip and dragged her further into a darkened room. She could smell chemicals and saw some cleaning supplies on shelves.

The voice in her ear was raspy. "I found you. I told you; you can't run from me. I'll find you anywhere. Where is she?"

Ginny tried to bite the man's hand and managed to get a piece of skin. She felt herself spin and a hand crack across her face. She fell to her knees and attempted to crawl away. Then she felt the man's hand on her ankle and pulled her flat. He slammed her face into the floor, and she felt the bone in her cheek snap.

Her attacker flipped her to her back, a large hand coming around her throat. A second hand slapped over her mouth when she tried to scream.

Rank breath assaulted her. "Where is she?"

Ginny choked, the large man's hand and body crushing

the air out of her. With barely enough breath, she said, "I'll never tell you."

She felt the sweaty hand slap across her mouth. "Tsk. Tsk. I could go to the police and tell them what you did. Gwendolyn is a small price to pay for your freedom."

Ginny gave him a small nod. The moment his hand lifted, Ginny spit at him and screamed as loud as she could. He slapped her again and rose.

Before he turned and ran, his eyes found hers. "Next time, sweetheart, I won't be so nice. And there will be a next time."

Chapter Six

Ginny was a no-show. Trenton shouldn't have been surprised. But something in how she had looked at him before leaving made him think she would. But it was eleven, and not even a phone call.

Penny sat next to Trenton. "What do you think she wanted by coming here?"

Gideon responded. "Trouble."

Nash stood by the window, his back to the group. "She didn't look like trouble. And she has a reputation. It's not like she was an imposter showing up pretending to be Ginny Page."

Isaac sat away from everyone else, legs crossed in front of him. "I thought it was odd she wanted to interview me. I should have followed my gut."

Nash interrupted. "Don't blame yourself. Why wouldn't she want to interview you? You're brilliant. But all I saw was free publicity."

Trenton glanced down at Penny, who was smiling at him encouragingly. "All I saw was a desirable woman. So we can all take some blame. Well, except for Gideon and Penny."

Gideon dropped down next to his wife. "I'll take some of the blame. I should have tossed her out when I found her trespassing."

Trenton laughed. "Penny, would you like to accept some blame, too? You didn't meet her, but you did let Gideon come pick me up last night, so it could be your fault, too."

Penny bumped shoulders with him. "Nah. But I wish I could meet her. I'd give her a piece of my mind."

Isaac peered at Penny over his glasses. "I think you would have, too. I do love having you as part of the group, Penny."

Penny's eyes softened. "You'll always be the quartet. Just plus one. And think, one day all of you will get married. What do you call eight?"

Isaac chimed in. "Octad."

Trenton groaned. "You would know the answer to that. But I'm swearing off women for a while."

Nash shuddered. "Especially if she is your sister. I can't even imagine."

Penny made a sound that sounded like a gag. "That's gross. Regardless of her reasons, I hope she is not your sister."

Trenton looked around the group. "Do all of you think I slept with her?"

Penny blushed. Isaac pretended to be interested in the nap of his pants. Nash kept his back turned so no one could see his reaction.

"Well, I don't." Gideon leaned over and slapped him on the knee.

Trenton's shoulders drooped. "Okay. So she knows who I was. It doesn't change much. But she didn't leave that book in my car. So who was the warning for? Her or me?"

Gideon contemplated that. "It was your car, so I guess

you. Maybe it was meant to scare you away. Whoever left it wanted you to know she is a liar."

Penny interjected. "Does that mean whoever left the book doesn't know who Trenton used to be?"

Isaac's head tipped in thought. "If we believe the book was meant to scare Trenton away, then I would say they don't know who he was. Ginny Page is famous in her sphere. It could be someone who doesn't like her books. Or doesn't like her perceived politics. This is D.C. after all."

Gideon rose and joined Nash at the window. "I'll be glad to see the last of her. I am glad, Nash, that you weren't the reason she was here. And Trenton, you're right. Who would care who you were? If people were to find out, it doesn't change anything for you. You were a kid. It's not like you were running the show."

Trenton hated this. "All we're doing is going around in circles. I don't know why Ginny sought me out. I don't know why she or anyone else would care about my past. I was a kid. But so was Ginny. If she's writing a book on the cult, trying to expose them, it's possible she thought I could be involved. My father was the leader. But he's dead. The cult is dead."

A soft voice came from the doorway. "I wish that were true."

* * *

If her face didn't hurt, she might have smiled. Five heads all jerked her way in unison when she spoke.

Trenton rose from the couch. "What happened?"

Ginny almost cried when he came to her and tipped her head toward the light coming from the window. "I had a run-in with a friend last night."

Gideon circled the room, forcing Ginny to come further inside. "Some friend. All your friends take fists to you?"

Ginny swallowed and gently pulled away from Trenton. "A couple. Can I sit?"

Penny jumped up from the couch. "Here."

Gideon growled at her. "Penny, she's the enemy here."

Penny ignored that. "Please, sit. Can I get you something? Ice?"

Ginny eased herself onto the couch. "You must be Penny. Sorry to meet like this."

Isaac didn't move from his spot. "Why are you here? I figured you'd be miles away by now."

"I'd say I'm sorry, but I wouldn't really mean it. But I do wish things had gone differently." Ginny fumbled with her bag and pulled out her laptop to open it.

Gideon slammed it closed. "I'm not interested in your book. I'm only going to tolerate your presence until we get some answers."

Trenton glanced at Gideon, who shook his head.

Gideon turned back to Ginny. "I'm in charge now. No more games. Why are you here?"

Ginny patted her laptop. "It would be easier to show you."

Gideon took a step back.

Ginny opened her laptop again. She pulled up the genealogy she'd been putting together. "When Jeremiah was killed, a good number of the members bolted. Mostly, they were afraid of the police or a raid. We all saw what happened in '93 in Waco. Some of the members wanted to stay and fight the police if they raided. Other scattered. I was young, but I remember my father grabbing my mom, who was pregnant with my brother, my sister, and me, and tossing us in a van with a bunch of others who were fleeing. It was like a caravan of cult refugees. There were probably close to a hundred of us then. Some dropped off as we crossed the country, but most stayed. We slept in campgrounds and I'm pretty sure the men robbed a few people to keep us going."

Trenton's eyes narrowed as he crossed to her. He looked at her screen. "You've been tracking the original cult members."

Ginny pulled up some photo collages. "The cult went on under a new leader. Jeremiah owned some land in Utah. His brother figured that with Elijah gone, he was now the heir."

Trenton's eyes closed. "Joshua."

Ginny nodded. "He set out to rebuild the cult, just like his father had done. He fancied himself Hezekiah reincarnated. Never mind that Hezekiah had been alive when he was born. Sometimes I think he believed it, but regardless, that's what he told those of us in his inner circle. That he was starting over again what had come before."

Penny came to see. "When did you leave?"

Ginny winced in pain when she tried to smile at Penny. "Six years ago."

Trenton began pacing. "When you became Ginny Page. I couldn't find any record of you before that."

Ginny leaned her throbbing head against the couch. "It was all a fluke. I lied my way into a job at a newspaper. I never had a job, but I was, sort of, the public relations manager of the cult. I wrote a lot of the propaganda Joshua printed. I wrote a bunch of fake publications and gave them to the hiring manager. I was shocked when she liked them. She didn't bother to verify any of them were authentic. For my first assignment, I was tagged to cover a social event where the actress Sonny Madison was going to be signing autographs and meeting fans. I wrote a very flattering article. Her agent reached out to me and asked if I was interested in doing her biography. I jumped at it. They paid me half up front."

Trenton stopped in front of her. "And Ginny Page was born."

Ginny closed her eyes. "Something like that."

Gideon grunted. "Why did the cult let you go?"

Eyes still closed, Ginny waved a hand over her face. "They didn't."

Nash swore from his spot at the window. "And you brought that mess into our lives without a second thought."

Penny crossed to her brother. "Nash."

"Don't 'Nash' me." Nash pointed a finger at Ginny. "Trenton has spent the last twenty-five years of his life forgetting those years. And you, without a second thought, bring that crap back into it. Who else did you tell? Who else knows who Trenton is? You can bet they'll have to get through us."

Ginny wanted to cry but held back her tears. She didn't expect sympathy, nor did she want it. Though right now, all she wanted to do was curl up on this couch and sleep. "Once I'm gone, no one will come. As far as anyone else is concerned, Ginny Page is interviewing a bestselling author and the founders of what will no doubt be the hottest game on the market next year."

Nash swore. "Except you aren't doing either of those things."

"It was my intent. But Cantwell and Isaac won't be the first projects of mine to be canceled."

Penny wasn't sold. "How can you be so sure they won't come after Trenton?"

"They're after me. I suppose they are after Elijah. But twenty-five years is a long time, and he was only eleven when he disappeared. And he's not the one trying to destroy them. Trenton Armstrong is a well-known public figure in D.C. He was part of one of the biggest financial firms in the city. Elijah is a kid who went missing in the aftermath of a collapsed cult."

Gideon pulled Penny to his side, calming and hushing her. "How did you find him?"

Ginny's swollen eyes opened. "I had a place to start."

Gideon took a step forward. "Where?"

Ginny sat up at his confrontational tone. "Genealogy. Joshua was tracing everyone's family line. Remember, Hezekiah was trying to make the perfect race of people. Joshua wanted to be his father, but perhaps not for all of the same reasons. I found the records Joshua was keeping."

Trenton turned back to her. "I doubt he let you see them."

Ginny shrugged. "I was snooping. Perhaps I had

reporter's instincts back then. I also had a digital camera. There was a teenager who lived near our property that would get you anything you wanted. For a price, of course. So I had a camera. I wasn't sure what I was looking at, but I took lots of pictures. When I decided I was going to expose the cult, I remembered the pictures. I was able to track Trenton down through his mother's family. Same way the police did. I didn't have pictures of Sarah, but I knew Jeremiah and Joshua looked a lot alike. But Trenton doesn't look anything like either of them. So I wasn't sure at first. It took a bit more digging to find any mention of an adoption in the family. Once I found that, I knew I had found Elijah."

Trenton swore and slammed his palm against the wall. "So there are records out there."

Ginny had as much as she could take. And if she went any further with her story, Gideon was apt to arrest her. So she rose, grabbing her bag. "No records. There was a fire. A big fire. Everything Joshua owned was lost that day, including Joshua. The only records are the old photos I have. They are not in a cloud anywhere. There is a mention of Elijah on my version of the genealogy, as well as many other names. They are all marked 'lost.'"

Gideon blocked her way when she would have left. "And your face?"

She clutched her bag to her chest. "Like I said, I ran into a friend. And I'd like to keep that from happening again. All of you can forget you ever met me. And you can be assured that one of two things will happen."

Gideon didn't step aside. "What are those things?"

She bared her teeth, and the words clenched through them. "I'll either be dead, or the truth about the cult will come out."

Penny laid a hand on Gideon's shoulder. He stepped back.

Ginny looked around the room. She didn't say another word; she just left.

* * *

Penny stared at the door. "So that's it? We let her walk? She's in no condition to be driving."

Trenton looked out the window. "No car."

Gideon closed his eyes for a second. "Go on. Go get her. Penny's right. We can't just let her go. I don't know who this friend of hers is, but he did a number on her."

Trenton looked at his friends. He nodded at them and ran out the door. Ginny hadn't made it far. He jogged the distance to catch up. "Where are you going?"

Ginny opened her mouth, but the words weren't coherent. "Gone."

Trenton saw her sway on her feet. He scooped her up. She fought him, but she was in no condition to win. "Stop. We'll go back to my house. I don't want you around my family."

Ginny's eyes closed, and she sagged in his arms. "Family. I want my family."

Trenton saw the tears that dripped down her cheeks. Cursing, he carried her up the porch stairs to Nash's house. "She needs help."

Ginny heard that and began struggling in earnest. "No. No hospital. Please."

Nash pointed to the hall. "There is a room in the back. Put her there."

Trenton laid her down on the guest bed. She looked small and pale lying on the white blanket. Her face, now that he was getting a closer look, was swollen to the point where her left eye was partially closed. She was lucky she still had her teeth. And that wasn't all. When he held her head to ease her down, he felt the knot on the back of her head.

Ginny grabbed his hand. There was barely any strength in it. "I'm so sorry. Wasn't supposed to be like this."

He didn't respond when he realized she had drifted off to sleep. He unwrapped the bag she had clutched to her chest from under her arms and set it on the bed. He pulled off her shoes and settled her under the covers. He then took the bag to the dresser. With no guilt, he opened it. Her laptop and tablet were there. Her wallet held a driver's license, issued to a Gentiana Lucinda Page, and a credit card in the same name. At the bottom was a thick pouch. His eyes narrowed on her after he opened it. It was filled with cash.

Trenton put everything back and closed the door. Everyone was looking at him when he returned. "She's out. I would bet money that her face is fractured, and she has a concussion."

Gideon ran a hand through his hair. "I called the station. There was nothing called in on a police report filed for an attack on Ginny Page. Or any other woman, for that matter."

Trenton glanced at the door. "She didn't lie about her name. I saw her license. Unless it's fake."

Isaac rose and came to his friend, putting a hand on his shoulder. "There is more to her story."

Trenton nodded. "I know. But somehow, I get the feeling she isn't going to share."

Gideon wanted answers. "Who was Joshua? She made it sound like he's dead."

Trenton drew back into his memory. "By blood, he was my uncle. Hezekiah preferred Jeremiah over all his other children. Joshua was born to a different woman ten years after my father. I don't remember Joshua much. He's a vague memory. But it makes sense. Jeremiah had been groomed since birth to take over. No doubt there was some rivalry. And jealousy. With Jeremiah gone, Joshua would have been the heir."

Penny came and joined her husband, then Nash. A circle of family surrounded Trenton.

Gideon shook his head. "In the family line, you would be next in line. But you disappeared. If she's lying, and they're looking for you, you could be in danger. No doubt they would want to shut her up, but you would be the prize at the end."

Penny looked at her husband. "But to what end?"

Trenton answered. "Money. It always comes down to money. If there are still cult members out there, they could be looking to find any threats. A long-lost son could be a problem. All of the wealth and possessions would be in the new cult leader's name. So if everything transferred from Hezekiah to Jeremiah to Joshua and then to whoever took over after Joshua, I would be a threat to that person. I would legally have the right to contest whatever he inherited."

Penny shuddered. "But Elijah doesn't exist."

Trenton tried to reassure her. "Only on paper. I wouldn't want a cent of that money. The worst years of my life were in that cult, surrounded by crazy sycophants."

Gideon stopped the thought. "Next step is to get a DNA swab from her. Now is probably the perfect time. We're not looking to use it in court, so it doesn't matter how we obtain it. And then I want to do some digging."

Penny seconded that. "Give me the swab and I'll go get it. But what are you going to do with her?"

That was the question, Trenton thought. He didn't know where she might go, or who was out there looking for her. But if that was what a friend did to her, he feared what an enemy might do.

Isaac spoke, "I can see those wheels turning, my friend."

Gideon came back with a DNA swab and handed it to Penny. He followed her. When they returned, he bagged it. "Penny and I are heading out. I'll drop this off at the lab. I just need yours."

Trenton took the swab and scraped the inside of his cheek. "I'll pay to put a rush on that."

Gideon nodded. He waited for Penny, who hugged Trenton. She whispered in his ear. "Be safe."

"I plan to."

Nash laid a hand on his friend's shoulder. "When she wakes up, I figure you'll take her with you. Just holler when you do."

Nash gave him a quick hug and went upstairs.

Isaac contemplated his friend. "And then there were two. You believe her; I can tell."

Trenton rubbed his chest. "The damn brand. Isaac, six years is not a long time to be out of a cult. If she's telling the truth and she's trying to expose them, she's in real danger."

Isaac gestured for him to sit. He did the same. "So she has the brand, and she knows your history. If Joshua had written everything down, she could have read it. It would be like a man like him to document every aspect of his life for posterity. History survives, even when the people do not."

"Her fear was real, Isaac. You can't fake that. It wasn't unusual for girls as young as fourteen to have a baby. My mother was only fifteen when I was born. I remember my father telling me that women were property. That they had to be controlled. I saw my father assault young girls. He would say he couldn't wait until I was old enough. I survived him, Isaac. And it's because of all of you that I did."

Isaac looked up at the ceiling. "Damsel in distress."

Trenton breathed a sigh of relief that he understood. "What if she's mine?"

Isaac shook his head. "It's just a story, Trenton."

Trenton couldn't shake the thought. "Penny was Gideon's. Lilah might be yours. We don't know about Nash yet. But what if she is?"

Isaac hummed. "Those paintings."

Trenton nodded. "A slender brunette."

Isaac sat back. "Gideon and his dreams. He dreamed the phoenix on your chest. He dreamed Penny. Let me guess, why not you?"

Trenton nudged his friend. "I noticed you didn't argue about Lilah."

Isaac straightened his glasses and rose. "Maybe she's for Nash, and some unknown blonde is for me."

Trenton knew Isaac didn't believe that. He didn't, either. Lilah was for Isaac. It would remain to be seen if Isaac ever admitted it. Or did anything about it. Lilah didn't particularly like Isaac, so Trenton could understand his skepticism.

Gideon had drawn four women after he had dreamed them the night after he'd read Isaac's book. He hadn't been able to sleep after the dream, so he had spent the night drawing them. He had set them aside. The drawings came to light when Lilah decided to draw all four men and turn them into the heroes in the game. None of them had been thrilled at first, but the renderings were so amazing that all four of them agreed to it. Then Gideon shared his drawings. They were done with chalk and pencils, and all four men, and even Lilah, knew they were perfect for the game. You couldn't see their faces; each woman's back was turned, as if being captured in a snapshot. That hadn't deterred Lilah. The women were in the mist during the game and only came in dreams.

Penny had been stunned to see the portraits. He and Isaac hadn't been there, but Nash had told them the story. She had known to whom each woman belonged. And she knew she was the woman in the portrait who belonged to Gideon.

Trenton's gaze went down the hall. He wasn't sure he

wanted her to be the woman in the portrait. Despite what he'd said to Isaac, he wasn't sure he believed the first painting was of Penny, no matter how convinced she was that it was her. But he knew what he did want. He wanted Ginny. And he hoped like hell she wasn't his sister.

Chapter Seven

Ginny hadn't thought she could feel any worse than she had when she left the hospital, but she was wrong. Evening light filtered through the curtains when she woke. Her head throbbed, and the nausea she had thought gone came back with a vengeance. She hadn't eaten anything in twenty-four hours, but even the thought of eating made her stomach heave.

She carefully sat up. Then she panicked. Her gaze flew around the room until she saw her bag on the dresser. She willed herself to slow her breathing. She was wobbly on her feet, but she managed to stay upright. She opened the bag and was relieved when everything was there.

First thing, she needed a bathroom. Second, she needed a plan. She'd lied to the nurse and the doctor and said she'd fallen. They hadn't believed her. She'd left the hospital against medical advice because she knew the longer she was there, the greater the risk. Since she'd gotten to the hospital by ambulance, she'd called a cab service to come get her and paid cash for the driver to take her to Nash's. She couldn't go back to the hotel. No doubt it was being watched. Her car was a rental, so the plan was to call and tell them where it was. Worst case, she'd pay for a tow.

She tossed her bag over her shoulder. The hallway, thankfully, led to a bathroom. She gasped when she saw her face in the mirror. The doctor had reset the bone in her face. He had sounded confident that she didn't need surgery. But wouldn't that have been her luck if she'd needed pins and screws in her face?

She gazed longingly at the shower. Her clothes were the same ones she'd worn on the boat. They were badly wrinkled. Thankfully she didn't have any cuts on her except for a busted lip. The final count was a split lip, a broken cheek, bruises on her face and knees, and a bump on her head. Though that bump was letting itself be known. Ignoring it, she carefully washed her face and neck with hand soap and left it at that.

She could see a lamp was on in the living room. She wasn't up to walking another gauntlet, but she supposed it was too much to hope that the house would be empty.

"Come on in, Ginny."

Ginny came around the corner. She sighed in relief when it was only Trenton. He had a tablet in his lap and was reading. "I hope Nash doesn't mind, but I used his bathroom."

Trenton watched her from his spot in the chair. "In your case, yes. But better than the alternative, no doubt."

Ginny flushed but stood her ground. "I just need to call a ride, and I'll get out of your hair. And Nash's."

Trenton rose. "Don't bother. I'll take you wherever you want to go."

Ginny watched as Trenton disappeared upstairs. She heard voices, two men and one woman. Instead of Trenton, it was Lilah who came downstairs.

Lilah's eyes widened. "Oh, my. They weren't kidding."

Ginny wobbled on her feet. She gripped the back of a chair to steady herself. "I'm a sight, for sure."

Lilah stayed where she was. "Trenton thought it might be a good idea if I stayed with you. I can drive you to a hotel. See that you get something to eat. A shower, maybe. I can't stay all night; I have to get home. But Trenton thought you'd be more comfortable with a woman helping you."

Ginny's knees buckled. She carefully wound herself around the chair so she could sit. "I'd say I hate to impose, but I could use your help. And a friendly face."

Lilah looked upstairs. "I'll be right back."

Ginny waited for Lilah to return. Trenton and Nash came with her. Ginny looked briefly at Nash, then averted her gaze. That one. He was the one whose fury was still very much on the surface.

* * *

Trenton was cursing himself the entire morning. He knew where Ginny was staying. Lilah had called him after she'd left Ginny in her hotel room. So instead of wiping his hands of her, here he was bringing her breakfast. Lilah had said she'd refused to eat. She'd accepted her help taking a shower, but that was it.

He knocked on the door. It was a minute before the door opened. Ginny, wrapped in a white robe, blocked the doorway. "I didn't expect you to show up."

Trenton took her arm and pushed his way into the room. "Can't say I was either. But here I am anyway."

Ginny closed the door behind her. "Is that coffee?"

Trenton set both bags down. He pulled two cups of coffee out of one, and two meals out of the other. He handed one to her.

Ginny took a seat, carefully folding the robe around her legs. "I guess I owe you for this. And for Lilah."

Trenton opened the first container. "I'll let you know when I decide what I want for payment. For now, I'll settle for you eating."

Ginny swallowed a sip of the coffee. She eyed the container.

Trenton handed her a fork and a napkin. "It's not liver, Ginny. It's just scrambled eggs and toast. Start with the toast."

Ginny stared at his hands as he put butter and jelly on her toast. She took a tentative bite. Then another. "Thank you, Trenton."

He opened his meal. "How do you feel?"

Ginny shrugged. "Better."

Trenton took a bite of his eggs. "You don't look it. For your sake, I hope you feel better than you look."

Ginny touched the bruise on her face. "Why are you here?"

Trenton wished he had an answer for her. But he didn't have one. He'd spent the night thinking about it. "I've decided to help you. My father was an evil man. I thought when he died, the cult died with him. Then you came into my life and told me otherwise. You hinted that Joshua was dead. But if someone is after you to silence you because you want to expose the cult, then that means the cult is still alive.

It's time to cut off its head and finish it."

Ginny sat quietly for a time. "You believe me?"

Trenton dumped four packets of sugar into his coffee while he spoke. "There was enough of the truth in it to be believable. I spent much of the night trying to figure out how you might benefit from lying to me about the cult. I couldn't come up with an answer. So if you weren't lying, then you were telling the truth. Though I have a feeling you left some pieces of your story out."

Ginny shrugged. "The rest of the story is mine. Maybe one day I'll share. But not today. So what is the next move?"

Trenton had been thinking about that, too. "Next move is to have you keep working on your piece for Cantwell. It's what you claimed you were going to do, so we might as well keep it as our cover story."

Ginny's heart rate picked up. "And Isaac?"

Trenton took a sip of his coffee. "That would be up to him. He wasn't too keen on the idea to start with, so don't hold your breath. Nash, on the other hand, was thrilled we were going to get free publicity for the game. It's the least you owe us."

Ginny tossed her toast back into the container. "I suppose I do. You've been friends with them for a long time."

"Since I got out of the cult. I told you; Isaac took me under his wing. I became part of the group."

Ginny leaned back in her seat. "And I brought it all rushing back. Nash was angry."

"You already know about Nash and his family's history.

He doesn't take kindly to threats against his family."

Ginny nodded but fell silent.

Trenton finished his coffee and breakfast. "Yesterday you said you wanted your family. Who are they?"

Ginny's eyes flew to his face. "I said what?"

Trenton started cleaning up their breakfast. "When I made you go back to Nash's. When I picked you up, you said you wanted your family."

Her gaze dropped to the table. "I don't remember."

Trenton stood abruptly. "If you're going to keep lying to me, we're not going to get far with your investigation."

Ginny looked up at him through her lashes. "I don't remember. Half of my family is dead."

Trenton came around and jerked her to her feet. "The truth, Ginny. I'm sick of this."

Ginny sagged in his arms. "The fire. They died in the fire. The same fire that killed Joshua."

Swearing, more at himself than her, he led her over to the bed and helped her lay down. She had turned white when he grabbed her. "You have a concussion. Why didn't you go to the hospital?"

Ginny rolled onto her side. "I did. But I couldn't risk staying. I had to get out. Too easy to find me."

Trenton took a seat on the bed. "How did the man who did that to you find you?"

Ginny kept her eyes closed. "Likely he's known where I am for a while. Ginny Page does get media attention. It was not a secret what my next assignment with the paper was. But I'm worth more alive than dead. He knows I hold the secrets that the cult would like to keep buried. As of yet,

I've not threatened them directly."

Trenton ran a hand through his hair, frustration eating at him. "And you have no idea who he is?"

"I know who he is. I just don't know his name. Once I know that secret, he'll come after me."

Trenton rose and paced the room. "We're going around in circles. Why not just take you out?"

Ginny opened her eyes. "Because if something happens to me, my boss will get all the evidence I've collected. It won't take him long to piece it together. He would then expose the cult. They've already had to start over twice. I don't think they believe they'll survive a third. For years, they've managed to stay under the radar. But if their secrets came to light, the FBI would be on them."

Trenton felt the coffee he drank trying to come up. "The children."

Ginny moaned and wrapped her arm around her stomach. "Yes, the children. Your mother was what, fifteen or sixteen? My mother was fourteen when she married my father. I was seventeen. The only reason I wasn't married off sooner was because of my brother. I helped take care of him."

Trenton didn't believe what he'd just heard. "You're married?"

Ginny pulled her knees tighter to her chest. "My lawyer says no. There were no legal filings. No one was legally married in the cult, not since Jeremiah. He and Hezekiah kept the marriages legal because Hezekiah wanted the children to be legitimate in the eyes of the church. But Joshua, despite wanting to rebuild the cult, didn't care about marriage or religion. No legal marriages would make it easier to stay under the radar."

Trenton thought back to the boat. He remembered her fear. Now he knew why. "You were forced to marry him."

"To be fair, so was he. He wasn't particularly thrilled with Joshua's choice in brides for him."

"His name?"

"Daniel Hamlin."

Trenton came back to her. "Where is he?"

Ginny's voice was faint. "Dead."

Trenton was torn between relief and rage. Relief because this man wouldn't be coming back into her life. And rage because he'd like to tear the man apart.

Trenton stood beside the bed as she drifted off to sleep. He watched her for a few more moments, then went to the table and opened her laptop. He'd watched her punch in her password. He started digging around her files.

While she slept, he copied all her files and uploaded them to his secured cloud storage. Eventually he'd turn it over to Gideon, but for now, he wanted to keep this between him and Ginny. None of his friends would approve of him helping her. And none of his friends wanted to see him hurt by dragging up the past. But it was too late to walk away from this, from Ginny.

Next, he pulled up the photo collages. Yesterday he had been relieved that his face wasn't among the images Ginny had. But front and center of one of them was his father. Jeremiah had been a handsome man. But what Trenton remembered most was how charismatic he was when he spoke to his followers. And how scary he was when he was alone with his father. Women came and went during the eleven years he lived with him. None of them lasted. None of them wanted to be his mother. So young Elijah had been isolated from the rest of the followers, with only a select few from the inner circle allowed to be around him.

Trenton rubbed his chest. He had just turned ten when his father had him branded. It was like he was declaring Elijah his heir. Ginny's brand was different from his, but no less frightening, given what it represented. He wanted to ask her how old she was when she got it. She had only been seven when Jeremiah was killed. He didn't remember there being any young girls in the inner circle.

Trenton closed up her laptop and set it back where she'd left it. She hadn't moved in the last two hours. And he still hadn't decided what to do about her. His baser instincts told him what he wanted to do with her, or rather to her. Self-preservation had him keeping his distance. Not only could she be his sister, but if a member of the cult was looking for her, he didn't want anyone to think there was more to her presence than a story. But he also felt a driving need to keep her hidden and safe. He wanted to bring her home with him and keep her there until they learned the name of the man hunting her.

* * *

When Ginny woke, Trenton was gone. She rubbed her eyes and moved slowly to her feet. When the room didn't sway, she made her way to the bathroom. She gently touched her cheek. It still hurt, but the swelling was starting to go down. The split in her lip still hurt, but it was looking better. All in all, she'd live.

She managed to shower and get dressed. Of course, the only thing she had to wear was the same clothes she'd been wearing for days. Lilah had kindly washed her undergarments for her, but the clothes were a loss. As she stood in the middle of her hotel room, she suddenly felt lost. She didn't know if she should stay or go. She didn't know if she should trust Trenton with any more of her secrets, or if she should run. Self-preservation said to run. Her heart was telling her to stay.

She went to her laptop and opened it. Tucked inside was a note written on a napkin. It simply said, "call me," with Trenton's name beneath. She glanced at her phone. She picked it up and dialed, but it wasn't Trenton she called.

"Hi, Levi. How's Gwenny doing?"

A soft voice came over the line. "The man hasn't shown up."

Ginny felt some of her tension fade. Ginny was pretty sure no one would find Levi and Gwenny. Ginny had been leaving enough breadcrumbs so that anyone looking for them would find her instead.

"I'll find him, Levi; I promise."

"And we always keep our promises."

Ginny smiled as tears gathered. "Yes, that's right. I miss both of you."

There were sounds of sniffles on the other end. "I want to go home, Gentiana."

Ginny closed her eyes. "Soon. Tell Gwenny I love her. I'll be in touch in a couple of days."

The line went dead without another word. She wiped the tears from her cheeks. She then dialed Trenton.

"Hello, Ginny. Feeling better?"

She swallowed and cleared her throat. "I'm better. Your note said to call. But I've been thinking that it might be better if I left."

"I'll just find you if you do."

Ginny held the phone away from her ear for a second. Then she gave up. "Fine. I'm not sure why you're all fired up to help me. Your friends are right. You should stay away from this."

Trenton's voice was loud over the line. "Then perhaps you shouldn't have shown up here, lied to me, and lied to my friends. But you did. And now we're going to do things my way. Pack up your stuff, and I'll be there to pick you up."

Ginny stared at the phone as the line went dead. She packed up her laptop and tucked her phone inside her bag. For good measure, she grabbed the travel toiletries from the bathroom and put them in her bag. She then took a seat to wait for Trenton.

Ginny was staring out the window when the knock came. She looked through the security peephole. Her heart ached at the sight of him. He was wearing tan slacks and a white button up shirt. His golden hair was styled, and he'd shaved. She opened the door right before he knocked again. She closed the door at her back.

Trenton frowned at her. "I should have had Lilah pick up some clothes."

Ginny hitched her bag higher on her shoulder, feeling

self-conscious. "All of my things are at the other hotel. Probably tossed by now."

Trenton grabbed her free hand. "Come on. I'm sure I have something at home you can wear until I can get to a store."

Ginny refused to move. "Home?"

Trenton yanked her forward until she had no choice but to walk. "Yes, home. I've decided to keep an eye on you while we figure out who this man is."

Ginny stopped fighting him and kept pace. "I call him the man in black."

"Johnny Cash?"

"Who?"

Trenton gave her a look of disbelief. "You don't know who Johnny Cash is?"

Ginny shook her head. "I've been in a cult since I was born, Trenton. So, sorry, no, I don't know who he is. A friend of yours?"

Trenton halted and looked at her. He touched a lock of her hair. "Six years."

Ginny slapped his hand away. "Six years, what?"

Trenton shook his head as if to clear it. He pulled her after him and hit the elevator button. "I was thinking the other day that six years isn't very many. I've been out for twenty-five."

Ginny realized what he meant. Some days were more of a struggle than others. When she'd gotten out, she didn't know what cell phones were, she didn't know how to dress like normal women, and she would often find people giving her the strangest looks. Not unlike the one Trenton had given her. Once she'd gotten accustomed to technology, she'd used it to learn as much about the world around her as she could. She still didn't know how she'd managed to land a job at the paper.

"How did you manage it? Getting free?"

Ginny pulled herself back from her thoughts. She was quiet until they exited the lobby. "A lawyer helped me. I'd gotten picked up by the police. I had no idea what a district attorney was. And I didn't know what else to do, so I told her where I came from. She knew of another lawyer who helped people like me."

Trenton opened the passenger door of his car. "What were you arrested for?"

Ginny's lashes lowered. "None of the charges stuck."

Trenton blocked her way. "That's not an answer."

Ginny stepped back from him. "It's the only one you're going to get. I'm not sure how you think this arrangement is going to work, but my personal business is my own. I'm sorry that I know so much about your past. But you don't see me dissecting your present."

Trenton stepped back, and she slid into the passenger seat. Her head was throbbing, and she wasn't up to sparring with him right now.

Trenton was quiet for a time as they drove. "Relax, Ginny. I won't bother you anymore today."

Ginny saw him glancing her way as he drove. "Thank you."

"Uh huh. But I will ask again."

Ginny closed her eyes, willing the ache in her head to quiet.

Chapter Eight

Ginny sat at Nash's kitchen table and took notes on her laptop as she interviewed Lilah. "How did you get involved in the project?"

Lilah had her head at an angle to see what Ginny was writing. "Nash. He knew some people in the gaming industry. When he decided to create a new role-playing game, he wanted someone with a lot of experience to help him build out the game without involving a huge team of people. A mutual friend gave him my name. We're at the stage now where we need people, so he's letting me head up a handpicked group to continue the development. He's on the hunt for a composer right now. He wants to make sure the music and sound bring the game to life."

Ginny rubbed the ache in her forehead but kept on going. "Trenton mentioned you'd been fired from your previous job when Nash approached you. But I'm guessing, regardless, you would have jumped at the opportunity."

Lilah fidgeted in her seat. "Well, sure. I mean, at first, I wasn't sure. I was a little nervous about working with four men. A girl can't be too careful these days. But the guys are great."

Ginny stopped typing for a second. "Even Isaac?"

Lilah stopped fidgeting. "He's fine."

Ginny's instincts told her there was something there.

"He's a brilliant man. He speaks fifteen languages. He reads dead languages. And to top it off, he's a very accomplished author."

Lilah glanced at the open doorway. She'd agreed to do the interview, but only at Cantwell's office. "He is brilliant. And accomplished. And rich. And handsome. He's practically perfect."

Ginny leaned back in her seat. "If you didn't say that so sarcastically, I'd agree with you. Up to the practically perfect part. No one is perfect."

Lilah wrapped her arms around her waist. "He just rubs me the wrong way, that's all. There isn't anything wrong with him. And he is nice."

Ginny tapped her pen. "You also said handsome."

Lilah fidgeted in her seat. "Can we talk about something else? I don't want to talk about Isaac. I heard him say you're not doing the book on him anymore."

Ginny froze. "Yeah, well, he decided it was a bad idea. He'll be in my Cantwell article, but after that we're parting ways. And sorry for being pushy about Isaac. I like him. He's a bit stodgy, perhaps, but I admire him and his work."

Lilah frowned. "He intimidates me. But that's on me, not him. He really has been nice to me, even when I'm being a pain. He and Trenton are best friends. The whole quartet are best friends, but you can see the extra bond that Trenton and Isaac have, and Gideon and Nash have."

Ginny had noticed, too, in the brief amount of time she had spent with all the men. "It's nice. I don't have close friends like that."

Lilah's shoulders dropped. "Same. But the guys are

great. I'm going to be sad when the job ends. They won't need me much longer. Nash is a lot savvier with a computer than he lets on. And I've done enough artwork for the game to spawn hundreds of side quests."

Ginny was surprised. "You won't be staying on with the company?"

Lilah kept her head down. "Like I said, they won't need me much longer."

Ginny wanted to press but saw Trenton in the doorway. "Hi."

Lilah spun in her seat. She got to her feet. "Trenton."

Trenton kept his eyes on Lilah. "We'll talk about that later. But Nash is looking for you. I thought I'd give you a rest."

Lilah started to head for Nash's office, but then stopped. "It's true, you know."

Trenton just shook his head.

Ginny closed her laptop. "She really is a sweet girl."

Trenton glanced back at the office doorway. "Not a girl. She's thirty. Life's been rough for her. She doesn't talk about it much. I don't suppose she confided in you?"

Ginny bit her lip. "No. I didn't want to push her too hard. It's not exactly relevant to the article. But there is something sad in her eyes. She hides it well. She was full of enthusiasm as she talked about the game, her first impressions of the story, and the artwork she says that Gideon did. And she's a fan of your photography. Can't say I blame her. You're very good."

Trenton rolled his shoulders. "Just a hobby. Did she show you the artwork Gideon did?"

Ginny shook her head. "She said it wasn't for her to show me. She said even Penny isn't allowed to see it."

Trenton came and took her hand. "Penny has seen some of it. Nash keeps most of it under lock and key. But the portraits aren't a secret."

Ginny trailed behind Trenton, and he led her to a room upstairs in the back. On one wall were portraits of the men. Her eyes went first to Trenton's likeness before glancing at the others. "Lilah said they were computer generated, but they look almost real."

"She did an amazing job with them. Gideon did these."

Ginny walked to the other side of the room. The art featured four women, each one facing away from the artist. First there was a golden-haired blonde. You could only see a sliver of her face. "Is that Penny?"

Trenton came to her side. "Penny says it is. Gideon will tell you he dreamed these women. So I would say it is her. Gideon has loved Penny for a long time."

Ginny's eyes came to rest on the second portrait. She lifted her fingers and traced the lines of the woman's hair. The woman wore a white dress with ties in the back. Her brunette hair hung down her back. Ginny's voice was a whisper when she spoke. "Who is she?"

Trenton laid a hand on Ginny's shoulder. "She's mine."

Ginny jerked out from under his hand. "What do you mean, yours?"

Trenton took a step closer. "The first one is Gideon's. The third is Isaac's. And the fourth is Nash's. The second one is mine. These are the women that the men are searching for in the game. The women they have to save."

Ginny felt her mouth go dry. His eyes bore into hers, and she felt like she was falling. She took a hasty step back in retreat. "Yours. Got it."

The intensity in Trenton's eyes faded. "Mine. So what do you think?"

Ginny got a grip. The woman in the portrait looked a lot like her from the back. But no way was she the woman Gideon dreamed. "I think these are lovely. So a redhead for Isaac, huh? Is that what has Lilah so wound up when it comes to him? Does she think she's his?"

Trenton leaned his hip against the nearby desk. "Penny says it's Lilah. Lilah scoffed and brushed it off. But it does make one wonder."

Ginny glanced past Trenton to make sure she didn't see Lilah. "She said he intimidates her."

Trenton glanced behind him. "Isaac? That's a new one."

Ginny turned her gaze back to the portraits of the men Lilah created. "He looks pretty intimidating in that picture. I wonder if that's how she sees him."

The portrait of Isaac showed a very powerful man. And like the other men, he bore the scars of battle. He had what looked like burns on his face around his right eye.

"Couldn't resist showing her, huh?" Nash stood in the doorway. He didn't look pleased.

Trenton turned to his friend. "She's already read the book. I thought these would bring it more to life."

Ginny touched the brunette's dress. "These certainly do. But don't worry, I don't have a camera on me."

Nash crossed his arms over his chest. "No cell phone?"

Ginny wasn't listening. When Nash called her name, her

head jerked. "What?"

Nash tapped her pocket. "Cell phone. I had better not see you taking pictures."

Ginny's gaze dropped to her pocket. "Oh, right. Cell phone. It's off. Just in case."

Gideon popped his head into the room. "Hey, Trenton. I need to talk to you."

Ginny shifted so that she was facing away from Gideon. Of the three men, he made her the most nervous. She didn't trust cops, and this one in particular was only tolerating her presence.

Trenton glanced back at Ginny. "Penny is on her way over. She said she would take you shopping."

Ginny looked down at herself. Trenton had lent her a shirt that was way too big. He'd washed her clothes, but she tossed the shirt. So she had the gray polo tucked into her linen pants and the sleeves folded.

Nash stayed behind. "So what do you think?"

Ginny gestured at the artwork. "I think Gideon is very talented. Lilah, too. You're lucky to have her. Lilah says you're good with computers."

Nash leaned against the door jam. "I'm fair. Why?"

Ginny bit her lip, then figured she had nothing to lose. "Trenton wants to help me. But you were the most vocal that I should get out of his life. I was thinking that if you helped, I'd get out much faster."

Nash's face was unreadable. "Is that what you're doing? Finding the man who did that to you so you can get out of Trenton's life? You've had ample chances to leave."

Ginny flushed but stood her ground. "He threatened to

find me. And let's be honest, Ginny Page isn't that hard to find."

Ginny could see Nash was thinking through what she said. He cursed. "I knew it."

Ginny followed him as he left the room. "Knew what?"

Nash turned on her, and she had to stop short to not run into him. There was fury on his face. "I knew he wasn't going to let this go. It had been years since he thought about the cult. We made sure of it. But you strolled into his life and stirred up all the old memories. Memories of his dead mother, beaten to death by a lunatic who just so happens to be his father."

Ginny swallowed the bile that came up. "How do you know his mother was beaten to death?"

Nash pointed his finger to where Trenton and Gideon were chatting outside. "He saw pictures of her that the police took. He has lived with those images in his head since he was eleven years old. And how do you think he felt when you showed up here, your face busted up and your eye swollen shut?"

Ginny swayed for a second. "Then help me. Help Trenton. Help him get closure."

Nash growled at her. "And in turn, help you. I don't think altruism is your strong suit."

Penny came cautiously into the room. "Nash?"

Nash scrubbed his hands over his face. "I'm fine. I'm just tired."

Ginny couldn't miss the concern on Penny's face as Nash left the room. "We don't have to go shopping."

Penny watched Nash until he was out of sight. She

turned watchful eyes to Ginny. "It's fine. Lilah is going to come, too. I think the men need some time alone."

Ginny nodded and went to grab her things. She glanced out the window where Gideon and Trenton were still talking. Nash joined them. She had no doubt they were talking about her, but she didn't think she wanted to know what they were saying. Penny was right. Let the men be alone. She tucked her laptop and notebook in the bag. And she tossed her cell phone in there, too.

Lilah came around the corner. "Ready?"

Eyes still on the men, she nodded. But Ginny didn't think she was.

*   *   *

The store was crowded, and Ginny felt like everyone there was staring at her. She had attempted to cover up the bruises on her face, but concealer hadn't done a great job hiding them. Penny and Lilah were going through the racks while she sat in a nearby chair. Her energy was lagging, and her head was still aching.

Lilah came and sat beside her. "You must be feeling awful."

Ginny shrugged. "I'll live. I'm just glad Penny is enjoying herself. Though I don't think this is a store she normally shops at."

Lilah tipped her head and watched Penny. "No. She's so classy. I imagine all her clothes come from specialty boutiques. Most of my stuff comes from thrift stores."

Ginny couldn't contain the memories. "I remember

making my own clothes. My husband's, too. We weren't allowed out of town to shop. When I got out, I vowed I'd never make another outfit as long as I live."

Lilah laid a hand on top of Ginny's knee. "I can't even imagine growing up in a cult."

Ginny shrugged. "I didn't think of it as a cult until I was older. It was just how things were. I went to school, did homework, went to church, and played with the other kids. After my brother was born, a lot of that changed. I saw how he was treated. He wasn't as smart as the other boys his age, and he was picked on by the other kids. He was ostracized by the adults."

"He's why you left, isn't he?"

Ginny felt tears form as she nodded her head. "I think my father hated him. I couldn't understand how the church could treat my brother so abominably. I was afraid when he turned eighteen, they'd throw him out. So I started making plans. And I started to realize everything around me was a sham. I had been lied to my whole life."

Penny stopped in front of them. "I can't believe I didn't know Trenton had grown up that way. He hinted at it a few times, but I never pushed."

Lilah shook her head. "You can see his past occupies a lot of space inside him. It's a dark one."

Ginny shuddered. "It is. But if I have my way, that will change. But for now, let's get this done."

Penny and Lilah helped her try on the clothes they picked out, and within two hours they were back at Trenton's house while Lilah did laundry.

Lilah was reading through all the notes Ginny had on the

cult. "I know some people who could try to find this man in black. In this day and age, it's a sure bet he's online. The cult itself might be tech-free, but in order to operate a scam this size, he'd need a computer and internet."

That got Ginny's attention. She set the fork down. "I didn't think of that. But you're right. One of the first things I bought after I'd escaped and started working was a computer. You can't do anything these days without a phone or a computer of some kind. He's not going to use the library like I did. Too risky."

Lilah started typing. "I mean, he could use coffee shops or libraries, but like you said, it is risky. But sometimes you can find privacy in a crowd. Let me do a little more research, and I can reach out to some friends. There has to be a way to find him."

Ginny felt a stirring of excitement in her belly. "I asked Nash, but you probably have more contacts than he does."

Lilah dropped her head. "More who are willing to bend the laws than his, anyway. I know people who know people. With Gideon around, I doubt Nash knows some of the less scrupulous folks out there."

Penny came around and looked over Lilah's shoulder. "You might be surprised. But Nash might not be the best person to help. I'm really worried about him."

Lilah glanced up. "He looked pretty mad earlier. And I don't think he's sleeping much."

Penny started pacing the spacious dining room. "He's been struggling since Clara. He's trying to make sense out of something that doesn't. Now he's focused on Trenton. Again, trying to make sense out of something that doesn't."

Ginny rubbed her aching temples. "I wish I had never come."

Lilah disagreed. "What if the man in black eventually figured out who Trenton is? He would have had no warning."

Penny kept pacing. "And how awful for Trenton that we all now know his secrets."

Lilah's shoulders dropped. "You're family, so it's okay. I'm sorry I overheard. I'm sure he doesn't like it that outsiders know."

Ginny stood and went to the windows. "This is so messed up. I'm so sorry. I've been obsessed with finding out who the man in black is. And I want to destroy every last remnant of the cult. But this wasn't how it was supposed to go."

The room was silent for a time. Ginny was about to drop the curtain closed when she saw a shadowy figure standing across the street. The figure tipped an imaginary hat. Angry, frustrated, and fearful for the two other women in the room, Ginny snapped.

Ginny grabbed a wine bottle from a nearby rack and ran from the room. Penny shouted at her to come back, but she ignored her. She ran out the front door, looking around for the figure she had seen.

Ginny ran to the sidewalk. "Come out, you bastard."

Penny and Lilah, both brandishing wine bottles, ran to stand beside her.

Lilah stumbled a bit as she came to a halt. "I don't see anyone."

Ginny spun around, trying to catch a glimpse of him. "I

saw him. He was here."

Penny pulled out her cell phone and called Gideon. "Gideon. He was here. The man who's following Ginny. We came back to Trenton's."

Ginny could barely hear his voice on the line, but the tone was angry. "He was here. I saw him. I swear."

Lilah put an arm around Ginny. "Let's go back inside. It's safer."

Almost hysterical, Ginny yanked away and ran into the street. "Come out! I'll find you. I'm not afraid of you."

Behind some bushes a few houses over, there was a loud, masculine laugh. "You will be Gentiana. I promise."

Ginny started to turn toward the voice, but both women grabbed an arm and started dragging her back into the house.

Penny tried to reason with her. "He could have a gun. Or a knife. Please, Ginny, let's go inside. Lilah is right. Come on. Please."

Ginny felt tears rolling down her cheeks and let the women take her back inside. She kept her eyes on the bushes, trying to catch another glimpse of the man. Nothing.

Penny closed and locked the door behind them. She then set the alarm. "Come on. We'll wait for Gideon in the living room."

Ginny ran to the kitchen and started packing up her things. "I can't stay here. I have to go. I need my clothes."

Penny stood in the doorway, blocking her way to the laundry. "And do what? Go where? Last time he got his hands on you, he could have killed you."

Lilah rummaged through the kitchen looking for a wine opener. She found it and opened the bottle. She grabbed a glass and poured Ginny a drink. "Ginny, please sit. You're not thinking straight."

Ginny kept her bag clutched to her chest but took a seat. She took a sip from the glass with a hand that shook.

Penny came and sat next to her. "It's okay, Ginny. You're not alone."

Ginny took a deep breath and another sip. "I don't know how he found me so fast."

Lilah poured a small amount into two more glasses and joined them at the table. She handed one to Penny before taking a drink of hers. "He could be tracking your laptop. Even your phone. They never leave your side."

Ginny rubbed the spot where the brand was on her chest. "How would he do that? My laptop is never online. It's the only way to make sure my files don't get hacked. But my phone is on all the time."

Penny glanced at the bag. "There are ways to sweep for bugs or tracking devices. Maybe one was planted on you. I had one in my purse when I was kidnapped, and I didn't know it. It's how I was found."

Ginny loosened her grip on her bag and set it on the table. "Maybe. I had my bag with me when I was attacked. Before that, I'd only seen glimpses of the man. Or what if he has a whole bunch of people watching me and I don't know it? The people in the inner circle were allowed out of the town. At least the men were allowed."

The front door opened, and all three women shot to their feet.

Gideon was first in. "Penny!"

Penny set her glass down and ran to the front door. She hugged Gideon to her. "The man who's hunting Ginny was outside."

Trenton, Isaac, and Nash followed behind Gideon.

Isaac closed the door. "Are you sure you weren't jumping at shadows?"

Lilah walked in with Ginny to join them. "No, we weren't jumping at shadows like a bunch of useless women in a horror film."

Penny shot Lilah a small smile. "No. He spoke to us. He was not a figment of our imaginations."

Trenton hugged Penny, then Lilah. He then looked at Ginny. "I'm glad you were safe. You didn't see him earlier today while you were out shopping?"

Ginny shook her head. "There were so many people. I felt like people were staring at me, and they were. But it was the bruises on my face that they were looking at. No one seemed threatening."

Nash scrubbed his palms over his face. "We have to catch this guy."

Lilah spoke up. "I know some people. I'm going to reach out to them. They might be able to find this guy's electronic tracks."

Gideon shook his head. "Forget it. I don't need amateurs helping. I know someone at the precinct who will help."

Lilah crossed her arms over her chest. "I am not an amateur. And neither are the people I know. And they won't be hampered by having to follow police procedures."

Gideon took a step toward her. "Police procedure is how you arrest him. Not going rogue."

Lilah stood her ground. "Not following police procedure is how we'll find him, and then you can build your case by following procedure."

Nash stepped between them. "Right now, I don't care who finds him. How long do you think it's going to take for this guy to figure out who Trenton is?"

Ginny waved that away. "I'm here for a story."

Nash swore. "The only story you're after is the cult. And he knows it. And now he knows where Trenton lives. He'll get someone like Lilah's friends to figure out who we all are. And it won't take long to put the pieces together once this guy learns Trenton was adopted. You just pull the string from there."

Trenton slammed a hand on the side table. "Enough. I always knew there was a risk that someone could find me. I thought the cult was dead, but that doesn't mean all of my relatives were. Lilah, see what your friends can dig up. Gideon, ask your friend at the precinct. We need to find this guy and get him out of all our lives."

Penny came and wrapped her arms around Trenton. "You think this person could be family, don't you?"

Trenton placed a small kiss on top of her head before stepping away from her. "It's likely. There were a lot of us. It could be the son of a sister I don't know. It could be an uncle or a cousin."

Ginny shivered. "It could be anyone. That's the problem."

Trenton turned to her. "No. It has to be someone in the

inner circle. That narrows the list. You started putting a list of names together. We should take that list and figure out who else should be on it."

Ginny paused, then took a deep breath. "There are four families in the inner circle. I married into one of them. That's how I got there. My dad wasn't part of it. So it's not a blood relative of mine. The largest family was yours, of course. Hezekiah's lineage. But even if we concentrate on just your line, it's a lot of names."

"The family names?"

"There is the Hamlin family. That was my husband's family. There is the Stafford family, or Trenton's family. Then there is the Hardenbrook family and the Nichelson family. We're talking close to a hundred people. Many of them scattered at the same time I left. It's impossible for me to know who stayed and who left. Most of the people I have found are not willing to talk for fear of exposing themselves. Many fear retribution."

Gideon was texting as they spoke. "We'll start there. Let me take a couple of pictures of your list of names."

Ginny looked over at Trenton, who nodded at her. She went to her laptop and pulled up the files Gideon wanted to see. She tamped down the fear she felt as he snapped pictures of the genealogy she had put together.

Gideon took Penny's hand and looked at Trenton. "You have that gun, yes?"

Trenton nodded.

Gideon looked at Ginny, then back at Trenton. "Make sure it's loaded and don't let it out of your sight."

Trenton simply nodded again. "It's getting late. I don't

think there's anything more we can do tonight. We all need rest."

Isaac pointed at Nash. "Especially you. Why don't you come and spend the night at my house? You can read one of my books. You'll pass right out."

Penny snickered. "Sounds like a plan to me."

Nash relented. "Sure."

The group disbanded. Lilah was the last to leave. She came over and hugged Ginny. "You're not alone anymore."

Ginny held her tight; emotions she didn't have words for were choking her up. "Thank you, Lilah. I could use a friend."

Lilah smiled at Trenton, and he walked her to her car.

Ginny went to the laundry and grabbed her new clothes. Tomorrow, she thought. Tomorrow she'd sort this all out. But for now, she didn't think the man in black would be back tonight. And she needed a bed.

Trenton simply watched her as she grabbed her things from the kitchen and went upstairs to the room he had given her.

Tomorrow.

Chapter Nine

Trenton was in the kitchen, watching birds play in his backyard. Gideon had texted an hour earlier that the new forensic analyst at the precinct, Freya Jensen, had agreed to help after work hours. It was her day off, and she was already running names.

But the most important piece Freya came back with was the DNA tests. She told Gideon there was no way he and Ginny were blood relatives. There was not a single match in their profiles. When he was around her, he struggled to remember that there was a chance she was related. When Gideon gave him the news, he could only feel immense relief that she wasn't.

He turned when he heard Ginny's voice. Her phone was tucked against her ear, and she was taking notes on a pad. "Story is going well. I've sent you what I have. I think you'll be pleased. And no, I don't think Dr. Brandt is going to change his mind. It was a long shot anyway; you knew that."

Trenton smiled when Ginny rolled her eyes. This was Ginny Page. The woman he had admired, not the woman who had lied to him and brought danger into his life and that of his friends.

"I'm not sure how much longer I'll be here. I might take some time off from traveling. I've got a few stories on the burner. Yes, I'll send you my proposals. I will. Thanks, Ron."

Trenton handed her a cup of coffee. "Agent?"

"Boss, but my agent said pretty much the same things. But Ron is getting antsy. Normally I'd have delivered the story by now. I'm running out of excuses. I can't stall him for long. But the Cantwell story is mostly done. Lilah was a fount of information. Nash gave me a lot of one-word answers, so I've been taking some artistic liberties with him."

Trenton was worried about Nash. They all were. "He's got a lot on his mind. And he's not thrilled with you right now."

Ginny shuddered at the bitter taste of her coffee. "Or ever. I don't think any of your friends are particularly fond of me right now. Including you. And after last night, I'm sure Penny and Lilah will keep their distance."

Trenton contemplated her over his cup. "Lilah likes you."

Ginny shrugged. "One out of six isn't good odds."

Trenton leaned back against the counter. "You didn't say much last night."

"What is there to say? I don't know how he keeps finding me. Penny and Lilah said I should get a scanner and see if there are any bugs or trackers in my stuff. And I'm still deciding what I should do."

Trenton hopped up and sat on the counter. "We're going to do what you set out to do. Find this man and expose the cult."

Ginny set her coffee down and placed a hand over her

stomach. "Lilah seems to think her friends can find him. Or at least figure out who he is. Gideon was pretty mad."

Trenton saw the hand on her stomach. "Gideon is strictly by the book. Very black and white. It's an admirable trait. But I get the feeling you make the book up as you go."

Ginny dropped into the chair at the kitchen table. "It's not like I have a lot of choice. I don't know the rules. And I don't trust cops."

"Gideon can be trusted. But I understand the sentiment. But I'd like to know why."

"Why I don't like cops?"

Trenton nodded.

Ginny wrapped her arms around her waist. "The night I ran, I had two cops after me. Except they weren't just cops; they were also cult members. They were the inside men. The night is a blur. But in the end, half the town was on fire, and one of the cops was dead."

Trenton's eyes narrowed. "Dead?"

Ginny lifted a brow. "I didn't kill him. Though I know who did. My lawyer says it was self-defense. But somehow, I doubt the police saw it that way."

Trenton filed away that piece of information. "You said the town caught fire. What happened to it?"

Ginny shrugged. "Half of it burned. There were still a lot of houses, but the town center, the church, and most of the businesses went up in flames. I can tell you the town was rebuilt, but the man in black isn't there. Many members had nowhere else to go, so they chose to rebuild. After it happened, most of the buildings were condemned by the county. And with no leader, there wasn't much in the way of money; the town is half the size it used to be. Only the people inside the inner circle would have had the resources to fully rebuild, and most of them are nowhere to be found. But the outsiders managed to hang on."

Trenton went back to what she had said before. "Was it arson?"

"Depends on your definition of arson, I suppose. Within the town, there was a warehouse that stored lots of munitions. Guns, homemade pipe bombs, bullets, flares, and who knows what else. The whole night was chaotic. Like what happened with you, there were members who wanted out. The two officers fired the first shots. People thought the cops had come and that a raid had started. Within minutes, more shots were being fired, and someone had thrown one of the bombs. The side building where food was housed went up in flames. People started fighting back, but they didn't know who they were fighting. More cops eventually came when the fire department showed up, but by then, one of the inside cops was dead, people were injured, and the fire was out of control. I don't know what happened after that. I ran."

Trenton didn't like the gaps he was hearing. "Did you run alone? What happened to your husband? You said he was dead."

Ginny rose and headed for the door.

Trenton jumped down from the counter and quickly went to block her way out of the kitchen. "We finish this now."

Ginny tried to shove him out of her way, but he was

immovable. "I told you he was dead. He died in the fire."

Trenton took a step and forced her back into the kitchen. "Did you see his body? Are you sure?"

Ginny struggled to finish. The words stuck in her throat. "I saw him. He was badly burned. There is no way he survived them."

Trenton took her hands. They were ice cold. "He was still alive when you found him?"

Ginny laid her head on his chest. "God help me, yes. I left him there. He would have tried to stop me if he could."

Trenton wrapped his arms around her. "You didn't have a choice."

Ginny turned wet eyes to his. "Didn't I? I didn't hate him. We were two people forced together. He wasn't always kind. And there were times he hurt me. But that's how it was for all the women."

Trenton didn't say anything. He'd seen what his father did to his women. To his mother. "I would never hurt a woman."

The side of Ginny's mouth curled up. "No. You wouldn't."

Trenton lowered his mouth to hers. He stopped within a breath. When she didn't pull back, he kissed her. He'd been dying to kiss her for days. Now that he knew she wasn't his sister, the leash came off. He cupped her face with his hands and kissed her softly and slowly, letting her get reacquainted with his touch. His hands slid from her face to her shoulders, and then he slid his palms down her arms, taking her hands in his. He lifted them until she wrapped her arms around his neck.

Still kissing her, he lifted her by the waist and turned her until she was sitting on the counter. He didn't force any other intimacy other than his hands on her waist. When he broke off the kiss, she was trembling. But it wasn't with fear. "One day, Ginny, we'll finish this."

Ginny didn't pretend she didn't know what he meant. "I haven't been with anyone else but my husband."

Trenton brushed a tear from her cheek. "I know."

Ginny pushed his shoulders until he stepped back. She slid off her perch on the counter. "I don't know what to make of you. You should hate me."

Trenton dragged his thumb over her swollen bottom lip. "Impossible. I've got this crazy feeling you were made for me."

* * *

Ginny knew any other woman would have laughed at him or thought he was crazy. But she had been drawn to him since the moment she met him. She thought back to Gideon's pictures. "A brunette."

Trenton dropped his hand but didn't say anything else.

Ginny took a deep breath. "So now what do we do? Lilah is no doubt in touch with her friends. And Gideon has his analyst helping."

Trenton went to the fridge and started pulling out breakfast. "We eat. Then we wait. You can use my computer if you want. I'll be using the desktop I use for work, but you can use my laptop."

Ginny nodded. They found a rhythm in the kitchen and

got breakfast on the table in no time. He left her in the kitchen with his laptop and left. She knew he kept an office upstairs, though he hadn't shown it to her during her tour of the house. She'd taken a quick peek inside her first night. He had a bookcase filled with all sorts of books. But what had caught her attention was all the photos he'd taken and framed of his friends. She hadn't dared go past the doorway since he hadn't invited her in, but she could admit to being envious. Friends had always been in short supply. She wasn't sure if Trenton was her friend or what, but he certainly had filled some of the voids inside. And she knew it was going to hurt when she left.

Instead of using the laptop, she texted Lilah. She'd asked her if she could get one of those bug scanners Penny had mentioned. She then took a hot bath.

She was climbing out of the cooled water when she heard Trenton pass the door. "Lilah is here."

"Be right out." Ginny quickly dried off and pulled on one of the new dresses she'd bought. The bright floral pattern, puffy sleeves, and long skirt made her feel like a normal woman again. Ginny Page wore suits and blouses. Gentiana wore dresses and jeans with t-shirts.

She came down the stairs. She was ready to wave at Lilah when she noticed Trenton staring at her. Heat grew in the pit of her stomach, but he left before she could react.

"Wow. What I wouldn't give for a man to look at me like that."

Ginny jerked back to reality. "Like what?"

Lilah gestured to the doorway Trenton had occupied. "Like he wanted to make a feast of me. I'd heard about looks like that, but never actually seen one before."

Ginny frowned. "You and Trenton?"

Lilah's eyes widened. "Goodness, no. He's way out of my league. But we're friends. And he's helping me invest some of my money. My mom is sick, and I've been struggling to pay her bills. He's helping me build a cushion so I can take care of her."

Ginny smiled. "That's sweet."

Lilah's head dropped and she focused on the bag she was carrying. "More like a godsend. I don't know what I would have done without his help. Cantwell pays well, but it's not enough. I'm hoping to be able to afford a nurse one day to stay with her."

Ginny didn't want to pry. Lilah had tears in her eyes and was struggling not to shed them. "Did you get it?"

Lilah held up the small device. "Get your laptop and phone. And anything else you might have with you."

Ginny did as she was asked and came back with her purse and her bag. "I left everything else at the hotel. I was afraid to go back. I guess I should have, since he found me anyway. Guessing my clothes and things are long gone."

Lilah nodded but focused on reading the directions on how to use it. It almost looked like an old-school walkie-talkie.

Ginny was frustrated after Lilah had scanned all of her things. "Nothing?"

Lilah set the device to the side. "Nope. I'm sorry. I thought we would find something."

Ginny felt sick to her stomach. The other alternative was that she was being followed and didn't know it. The man in black didn't hide from her. He would appear, usually hiding behind a tree or a car. He'd let enough of himself be seen so there could be no mistake about who he was.

Lilah put the device back in the bag and left it. "I've got my friends looking into the names you gave me. And they are trying to track any financial records that can be tied to them or any shady businesses out of Utah. They'll message me if they find something. I'll let you know if I hear from them."

Ginny nodded, feeling numb now that the nausea had passed. "Thank you, Lilah. I don't know how I can repay you for this."

Lilah grabbed her bag. "No payment needed. It's the right thing to do."

Ginny gave her a quick hug. "I've been interviewing people for a few years now. Rarely do people do things because it's the right thing to do. They do things to benefit themselves."

"Then I feel sorry for them. I'll be in touch."

Ginny waited on the porch until Lilah was safely in her car and down the street. She glanced around, but she didn't see anyone. Frustrated, she closed the door. She pulled up the directions and read through them herself. She did a second scan. Nothing.

Ginny went back to what she was good at. A few hours later, she had finished her article on Cantwell. All four men and Lilah had contributed to the story. They were a unique bunch. She pulled up the picture she had taken of the men. Gideon was taller than the rest of them. You couldn't miss the scars, but somehow, they fit his personality. Isaac was somber. He was definitely a serious scholar, but his books showed that there was much more to the man than he showed the world. Nash was a mystery. Right now, everyone was walking on eggshells around him. She could sense there was a story there. She knew of his grandfather's death, but it had to be more. His visceral reactions to Penny's kidnapping and his cousin's death went well beyond what one would expect. But she had already caused enough trouble, so she set her curiosity aside.

And Trenton. He was all smiles. He was charming and oh so handsome. But she had meant it. She didn't understand him. It was never her intent to get this involved. When she had sought him out, she knew there were three possible scenarios: he was guilty, an accessory, or he was innocent. But her research proved he hadn't had any contact with the cult since his childhood. Had she had any sense, she would have lied to him and left. But her good sense seemed to have been absent since they met.

The kisses. They were so sweet. He'd not pushed her or rushed her. And he hadn't tried to pick up where they left off on the boat. But she knew he was right. She would end up in bed with him if she stayed. He made her forget herself; forget what had come before.

Daniel hadn't meant to hurt her, at least not in the beginning. She'd been too young and too inexperienced to understand what he was doing to her. And to be fair, he had been too. His father had taken him aside, no doubt explaining what marriage meant. For a time, things had been okay. They had fallen into what she supposed a marriage between two teenagers looked like. But as time had gone by, as they'd both grown older, she'd refused to conform to the cult's idea of a "perfect" wife. He had become angry and resentful toward her. And that's when he used his size and strength to try to force her into submission. But the more he tried, the more she fought.

She turned when she heard a sound. Trenton was watching her. "Are you okay?"

Ginny shook her head. "No. Lilah didn't find anything on me. I don't know how he keeps finding me. I'm scared. Scared that there are others watching me. Watching you."

Trenton came into the room. "I know where we can't be watched. Maybe disappearing for a little while would be good. Nash, Freya, and Lilah can keep digging. Gideon can do what Gideon does best and keep it all on the up and up."

"Where?"

Trenton went to the fridge and started pulling items out. "My boat. We'll have the radio and a satellite phone, so we won't be out of contact. I can't imagine this man would get his own boat and follow us. Out on the open waters, he's not going to be able to find us."

Ginny felt a shred of hope. "I'll go pack."

* * *

Trenton watched her retreating back. He pulled out his cell and called Gideon. He told him where they were going.

Gideon's voice was loud over the background noise of the precinct. "It's not a bad idea. Penny will second it. She's been worrying about you when she's not worrying about Nash."

Trenton glanced up the stairs. "I know. And I'm sorry. But I can't let this go."

Gideon grumbled but didn't argue. "At this point, the safest route is to expose the cult and end it for good. Nash is right. It wouldn't take much digging to put the pieces together that you're the missing heir."

Trenton put the phone on speaker and started packing up the groceries. "We'll be leaving here shortly. Ginny is packing. I'm getting supplies. I'll text when I leave the docks. Just let everyone know we're fine. And calm Isaac down. He's going to be furious."

Gideon grunted. "Nash, too. But it's a good plan until we can come up with a better one. But do me a favor."

Trenton zipped up the bag. "What's that?"

"Pack a damn box of condoms."

Trenton stared at the phone for a moment. Then smiled. "You got it, Boss."

Gideon laughed and hung up.

Trenton resumed packing. He then went upstairs to get his things. The first thing he did was tuck a new box of condoms into the bottom of his bag.

He quickly packed the rest of his things. He then went to find Ginny. He found her standing in the doorway of his office, the bag he'd given her to pack her stuff in at her feet.

He came up behind her. "What are you looking at?"

Ginny leaned back against him. "Pictures. I was thinking, other than the ones I have of the cult members, I don't have any pictures of my family. My father would have beaten me if he knew I had a digital camera. My husband, too. But I have no pictures of my mother or my sister and brother. My sister has a daughter, Gwenny. I don't have pictures of her either."

Trenton offered her what comfort he could. "You have lots of time to make new memories. And take lots of pictures."

Ginny smiled. "Not like these. You really do have a talent."

He took her hand and led her to the bookcase. "The first one is my aunt and uncle. The ones that took me in. They're great. They moved to Florida to be snowbirds, so I don't see them as much. I have lots of pictures of the quartet, though most were never printed. But the one you keep looking at, Penny took. I had just gotten the boat, and I took everyone out for an overnight cruise. Penny wanted to commemorate the moment."

Ginny glanced at him. "You are a handsome bunch. Did Penny always have eyes only for Gideon?"

Trenton touched a finger to the picture of Penny he had taken the year she graduated college. "Yeah. No other guy really stood a chance."

"You two are close, though. I can tell."

Trenton nodded. "She's one of the guys. Just prettier. Before she and Gideon got together, we spent a lot of time together. It was nice having a girlfriend that wasn't a 'girlfriend,' if you know what I mean."

Ginny touched the picture in the same spot Trenton had. "No sex."

Trenton smiled. "No sex. No desire for sex."

Ginny walked over to his desk. The computer was off,

but there was a notepad open. "Lilah said you've been helping her with her finances. She said her mom is sick."

"Very. I'd been thinking of leaving the firm for a long time. I made Lilah my first client."

Ginny ran her fingers down the figures. "These don't add up. There is way more money here."

Trenton laid a finger over her lips. "And that secret stays between you and me. Got that?"

Ginny nodded. "My lips are sealed. I told her you're sweet. This just proves it."

Trenton shifted uncomfortably. He didn't like the word sweet. It meant things like rainbows, flowers, and candy. Things that he was not. "The quartet helped me emotionally get back on my feet. And my aunt and uncle set me up financially. Just paying it forward."

Ginny took a step back. "We should go."

Trenton grabbed her bag and gestured for her to precede him.

Chapter Ten

The boat drifted along the waves. Ginny was drowsy but not yet ready to sleep. It was peaceful out on the water. The stars overhead seemed brighter than they ever had. In the city, you barely saw the stars. Within the cult's town limits, there were always harsh lights at night so everyone could be watched. But all of that seemed long ago. She felt relaxed for the first time in ages.

She had managed to sneak in a call to Levi and Gwenny before they sailed, so they knew she was okay and getting closer to coming home. But she didn't want them to worry when she didn't contact them for a few days. Gwenny was adjusting well to her new school, and she was making friends. It made Ginny feel like she was doing the right thing. She wished she could do the same for Levi. And one day she would. But today she needed him to be with Gwenny so she could finish what she had started.

She glanced over her shoulder. Trenton was on the top deck, lying on a cushioned bench. He said he was going to drop anchor soon, but for now, they were both enjoying the peace and quiet of the water. Trenton had opted to take them to the Atlantic. The trip down the Potomac River to Chesapeake Bay had been lovely, but being out on the ocean was a whole different experience for her. They were a few miles from shore, and everything looked so small. A little further out, and it would be as if civilization didn't exist.

The past two days, Trenton had been focused on sailing. They shared meals and talked some, but mostly she'd wandered the boat and caught up on her sleep. No one could find them here; he was right about that. She was feeling better than she had in ages, and she'd slept the past two nights like a baby.

It was nearly midnight when Trenton dropped anchor and went below to his room. Ginny had bid him goodnight but stayed where she was. She'd spent a lot of her time thinking about Trenton. It was hard not to when he was usually only a few feet away.

Propping her elbows on the railing, she closed her eyes. He had told her that she had lots of time to make memories. But did she? The man in black aside, she had seen how quickly life could be taken. She'd lost her parents and her husband in one day. And while she believed her sister was still alive, she had lost her that day, too.

Ginny stood and dropped her arms. She wanted to make memories. Good memories. She wanted Gwenny to grow up and live a normal life. She wanted Levi to move into the group home he'd been begging her to let him move into. But what did she want? When this was over, she knew she wanted to keep being Ginny Page. She liked her job. She liked wearing suits and spending hours researching and writing.

But right now, she wanted something else. She wanted Trenton. Trenton with his golden hair, broad chest, handsome face, and facetious smile. He was a memory she wanted. And here, away from the rest of the world, where she could pretend the past never was, was where she wanted to make those memories.

Ginny silently made her way inside. There was less light inside, but she could still see. Trenton kept the windows uncovered. She made her way to his bedroom. She eased open the door. He was lying on his stomach, with an arm curled under his pillow. His eyes were closed, and his breathing was even. She could see the naked skin of his back in the light from the moon.

She edged her way toward his bed. "Trenton?"

His eyes opened, and he sat up. "What's wrong?"

Ginny sat on the edge of the bed. "Nothing's wrong. But I think something might be very right."

Trenton rubbed his eyes. "It's really late, Ginny. I'm not in the mood for your word games."

Ginny stood up and glared at him. "Okay. No word games. I want to have sex."

That got his attention. "What did you say?"

Ginny sat back down. In the light, she saw the large phoenix tattoo on his chest. Over his heart. The bird was beautiful; its bright red and orange wings in flight. She touched it with the tips of her fingers. "It's beautiful."

Trenton laid a hand over hers. "Gideon drew it. You want to run that by me again?"

Ginny's fingers curled into the skin on his chest. His chest only had a small smattering of golden hair across it, but she could feel it tickling her palm. "I was thinking about what you said. I want to make memories."

"Ginny. Are you sure you're ready?"

She pressed her lips to his neck. "I'm sure."

Trenton scooted over to give her more room and tucked the sheet around his hips. "Then, come here."

Ginny shifted and swung her legs onto the bed. She waited and wasn't disappointed when his arm came around her hip and brought her closer to kiss her. She twisted so that she was slightly on her side, and her body was pressed to his. Face to face and hip to hip. She lifted a hand so that she could lay it over his heart.

They sat that way for a time. She relaxed as he did nothing more than kiss her. The kisses were light, brushing against her lips. But they became bolder, his lips opening her mouth to his. Her other hand fisted in his hair as his tongue touched hers, and she felt heat begin to build inside her.

Ginny broke the kiss for a moment. His eyes were hooded as they watched her. With hands that shook, she stripped off her t-shirt. Even though he had seen her brand before, it bothered her that he would see it again. Her hand stilled over her heart.

Trenton kissed her. "It's not what makes you who you are."

Ginny shivered as his hands came around and unhooked her bra. With her hand still over the brand, he managed to pull off her bra.

Trenton eased her onto her back. "I want to see you, Ginny."

She realized her arms were covering her breasts. She flushed but dropped her arms. She wanted this. And part of it was him seeing her. All of her.

She sighed when he didn't focus on the brand. With light

strokes, he caressed her breasts, his fingers dragging across her tight nipples. She arched her back at the pleasure of it. He wasn't grabbing at her, but he still seemed to enjoy what he was doing to her.

Trenton bent his head and kissed one nipple, then the other. "You're beautiful, Ginny."

He made her feel beautiful. He kissed his way up one breast to her collar bone. He then settled a hand between her thighs, not touching her, but making his presence known. He then kissed his way across her chest to her other breast. Her belly quivered when he kissed the underside of her breast, and his fingers kneaded her belly.

Ginny shifted and felt his arm against her core. She stilled but then shifted again to increase the pressure.

Trenton left his arm where it was and used his other hand to unsnap her jeans and pull the zipper. He kissed the skin over the edge of her underwear. His fingers drifted under the waistband and wrapped around her hip. She wriggled when his fingers found her backside and lifted her against his arm.

"Trenton." Ginny lifted up on her elbows so she could kiss him. She wanted to cry when he moved his arm, but his mouth crushed hers to his, and he used his grip to ease the jeans and underwear off her hips. She lifted up to help.

Trenton pulled away from her and sat on his knees. With both hands, he finished stripping her. She couldn't believe she was lying nude with a man. And then she realized he was naked. He had kept the sheet over his hips, but it had fallen away when he came to his knees. With a hand that trembled, she reached out to touch him. She kept her touch light, just the tips of her fingers exploring the feel of him.

"Ginny?"

She dropped her hand. "What?"

He lowered his brow to hers. "I don't know how much of that I can take."

Ginny didn't understand. "I shouldn't touch you?"

Trenton cursed under his breath and took her hand and brought it back to his flesh. "You can touch me. I want you to touch me. But damn, woman, that feels good."

She smiled at him. "Okay."

He laughed, but she knew he wasn't laughing at her. She moved her hand back to his chest. "Kiss me again."

Trenton lay back down and brought her body flush to his. He pulled her hips to his and let her get used to the feel of him against her. His voice was low and gruff. "It's just a different kind of kissing."

Ginny shivered. Her aching breasts were pressed firmly against his chest. She could feel his erection pressed up against her thigh. She knew what came next, of course. But this time it seemed like a pleasurable thing. She scooted until she was on her back. "Okay. I think I'm ready."

Trenton dropped his brow to hers. "Are you sure?"

She tensed when one of his thighs settled between her legs. She knew he felt it, and she was sorry for it. "Trenton, it's okay."

Trenton shook his head. "I've got a better idea."

Ginny watched as he stood up. She felt tears gather. She also felt herself flush with embarrassment. She sat up, unsure of what to do when he left the room.

She was half ready to flee when he came back. But she saw what was in his hand. "Oh, I forgot about that."

Trenton tore the condom packet open. "So did I."

Ginny went to lie back down, but his hands stopped her. "Don't you want me?"

Trenton swore and brushed the tear that rolled down her cheek. "I don't think I could want you any more than I do right this second. But I have a better idea."

Trenton took a couple of pillows and propped them up against the headboard. He lay down on his back and took her hands to pull her closer to him. "Now, come here."

Ginny obeyed. She felt his hands on her thighs, guiding one of hers between his. Her legs opened to his touch, and she thought she'd jump out of the bed when his fingers slid against her wet flesh. She remained still, her eyes closing at the feel of his hand between her thighs. Then instinctively she moved until she was sitting astride him, and his fingers delved further.

Trenton's breath was coming out in quick puffs. "Do you want me, Ginny?"

She nodded her head and tried to bring his fingers closer.

Trenton rolled the condom on. "Then come take me."

Ginny's eyes shot open. His hands were now on her hips, and he was gently urging her forward. Did she want him? Oh, yes. She rose up on her knees so that he could guide her hips. She felt just the tip of him ease into her. The feeling was amazing, and she savored it. But she wanted more. She eased herself slowly onto him until she couldn't take any more. She felt her insides quiver around him, the tension inside already unbearable.

Trenton grabbed her hips and eased her a little more forward. Then he shifted his hips until he was almost out of her, and then smoothly slid back in.

Ginny found the rhythm he set. She could feel her body straining toward him, the pressure inside her building. She flexed her hips one last time before succumbing to the overwhelming pleasure of her first orgasm. She was barely aware of him climaxing inside her; so great was her focus on the pleasure of her own body.

Ginny's body sagged against him, her thighs loosening. She smiled down at Trenton, who was watching her with hooded eyes. She then lay down on his chest so that her head tucked under his chin, but their bodies were still entwined. She kissed his damp chest, her head lying over his heart.

They were quiet for a time. Ginny wanted to stay where she was, but Trenton was shifting and separating their bodies.

"I'll be right back."

Ginny slid onto the sheets as he left the bed. She pulled a pillow and tucked it under her head. She had no desire to move.

Trenton came back and set two more condoms on the dresser. Then he pulled the sheet over her naked body and lay down beside her. He pulled her against him. "Feeling okay?"

Ginny scooted closer. "I'm tired now."

Trenton's chest shook slightly under her palm as he laughed. "That happens a lot after great sex."

She sighed. "It was, wasn't it?"

Trenton kissed the top of her head. "The best."

Ginny smiled, thinking this was the loveliest of memories she could have made. She then drifted off to sleep.

* * *

Trenton was humming while he made breakfast. That might be a first for him, he mused. He'd left Ginny sound asleep in his bed. He'd attempted to wake her and make use of the condoms on his side table, but she hadn't budged. She had snored softly against his chest, then turned to bury her face in the pillow and continued to sleep. He got up instead of waking her, pulled the shades to block the morning sun, and let her be.

While fixing breakfast, he kept an eye on the storm radar. There was a squall not far out that would arrive in the next hour or so. They would get a good wind and rain, but he wasn't worried. He was worried about Ginny, though. Her first time on the boat, she'd gotten sick. They were in for some rough waters this morning. Perhaps she'd sleep through it. He had noticed the dark circles under her eyes had lessened over the last couple of days. So had the bruises on her face. Minus some discoloration, they were mostly gone.

He fixed some pancakes and put them in the oven to keep warm and set about cutting up some fruit. He was just about finished when Ginny joined him. She was wearing another dress; this one molded her unconfined breasts and only hit the top of her knees. Unable to resist, he came over and kissed her. He meant for it to be a brief, soft kiss, but he was unable to stop with a brief caress. His hands slid over her hips and bottom, pulling her against him.

After a few moments, he let her go. "Good morning."

Ginny blushed. "Good morning to you."

Trenton smiled to himself as she took a seat. He couldn't help but admire her nipples pressed against the fabric.

Ginny crossed her arms over her chest. "I need coffee."

Trenton turned and poured her one. He handed it to her.

Ginny dropped her arms to grab the cup. With one last glance, he went back to fixing breakfast. Within minutes, he was setting two plates down and placing butter and syrup on the table.

Ginny skipped the butter but dug into her pancakes. "I'm starving."

Trenton popped a strawberry slice into his mouth. "I can't imagine why."

Ginny blushed. "I've not had a morning after before. I'm not sure what I'm supposed to say."

Trenton shrugged. "Anything you want. Or nothing. There are no hard and fast rules around it. But I would like you to relax."

He watched with amusement as she took a deep breath and her shoulders relaxed. He continued to eat.

Ginny was looking out at the water. "A little gloomy today."

Trenton sighed. Apparently, they were going to be reduced to talking about the weather instead of the great sex they'd had last night. And why she had suddenly shown up in his bedroom. "Storm is coming. Just a squall. It will be gone before you know it."

Ginny poured some more syrup on her pancakes. "So, did we start an affair last night?"

Trenton set his fork down. So, they were going to talk about it. "I suppose that's up to you."

Ginny spun her fork. "I've heard that sometimes men only want a woman once."

Trenton leaned over and tipped her chin up so she was looking at him. "Men are pigs. What can I say? But no, once was not enough. Twice won't be enough. So, to answer your question, yes, as far as I'm concerned, we started an affair."

Ginny smiled at him. "So can we do that again after breakfast?"

Trenton was glad he didn't have food in his mouth. He'd have choked on it. "Yeah. We can do that again after breakfast."

Trenton wasn't sure how he made it through the meal, but they finished it in record time. Then she insisted they clean up the mess in the kitchen. It was like there were two women inside her. But whichever one she chose to be in the moment, both turned him on.

Ginny put the last glass in the cabinet and turned. She let out a squeal when he picked her up but gave no protest.

Trenton laid her down on the mattress and stripped her of her dress. He then stripped. He took his time teasing her body into full arousal. And when she didn't stiffen beneath him, he donned the condom on the table, spread her thighs, and surged inside her. He loved the feel of her thighs squeezing him and her legs wrapped around him. And when she climaxed beneath him, he thought he'd died and gone to heaven.

* * *

Ginny listened to the rain and wind blowing around the boat. Trenton was dozing beside her. She lifted a hand to her neck. The skin was a little irritated, but she didn't mind. She had reveled in the feel of the beard that he was growing on board the boat as he nuzzled and bit the soft skin. She wondered if she had a hickey. If she did, it would be a first. She rolled onto her stomach and smiled at him. He was a first for a lot of things.

She was starting to doze when her phone chirped. Gwenny loved birds, so the ringtone was unmistakable. She slowly eased off the bed. She didn't want Trenton to wake up. She took her phone and went outside. They were close enough to the shore that she could still pick up cell service. She dialed.

"Levi? What is it?"

"Gwenny is sick."

Ginny could feel her heart as it leapt in her chest. "How sick? What's wrong?"

Gwenny took the phone. "Mommy, my tummy hurts."

Ginny took deep breaths. A tummy ache she could handle. "Did Uncle Levi give you some medicine?"

"Yeah. But it still hurts."

Ginny took a seat on the bench. "Want me to sing you a song?"

Gwenny's excited clap over the line was her answer.

Ginny kept the phone close to her ear as she sang Gwenny her favorite lullaby. "Feel better?"

Gwenny's voice was drooping. "Better. Love you, Mommy."

Ginny wiped a tear. "Love you, baby. Get some sleep for Uncle Levi. You'll feel better when you wake up."

"Bye." Gwenny's voice trailed off.

Ginny hit the end button.

"Mommy?"

Ginny spun in her seat. Trenton was behind her. He'd not bothered to put any clothes on before he sought her out. Of course, she was also sitting naked in the rain.

Trenton came toward her. "How many more secrets, Ginny? How many more lies?"

She couldn't help but hear the controlled anger in his voice. But he didn't give her a chance to answer. He turned and went inside, slamming the door to the cabin behind him. Ginny ran to the door and followed.

"I didn't lie."

Trenton kept his back to her. "Leave me alone, Ginny. I can't talk to you right now."

Ginny didn't follow a second time when he went to the bedroom and shut the door. She heard the shower come on. She dropped onto one of the sofas. Then she realized she was still naked. She went to her room and grabbed a different dress. She didn't dare go back into his bedroom. Not with the way he had looked at her. Buried beneath the anger had been pain. Pain she'd caused.

Unable to think of anything else, she texted Levi for a

favor. She smiled when he messaged her back. She couldn't keep this memory, but she could share it before deleting it.

She waited for him in the living area. The rain was now just a trickle, but she didn't venture back outside. She waited an hour. He came into the room. He was wearing an old pair of jeans and a fitted gray t-shirt. He didn't say a word.

She pulled up the photo on her phone and handed it to him. Gwenny's bright gold curls were in disarray around her face, and her huge smile showed she had lost another tooth.

Trenton took the phone and gazed at the girl. "How old is she?"

Ginny smiled. "Six and a half."

Trenton's hand tightened on the phone. "Why lie?"

Ginny's smile faded. "I didn't lie."

"This is Gwenny, isn't it? You said she was your niece."

Her legs felt like rubber, so she sat. "She is. But I'm also her mother. Not her biological one, but the only one she knows."

Trenton's lips tightened. "Then it amounts to the same thing."

Ginny's shoulders drooped. "I suppose you're right. But she's my secret. No one is supposed to know about her."

Trenton handed her back her phone. "I don't like the way you said that. Who knows about her?"

Ginny's hand trembled as she tucked the phone into her dress pocket. "The man knows. He was following her. He tried to take her. But Levi stopped him."

Trenton pulled up a kitchen chair and sat across from

her. "You said Uncle Levi. Your brother?"

"Yes. She's with him. I put them in a safe place. So far, no one has found them. Or at least, Levi hasn't seen anyone. And Levi's not a trusting sort, so he's always on the lookout for strangers."

Trenton rubbed his temple. "Why Ginny? I thought by now you trusted me."

Ginny wanted to reach out but didn't. "I do. But this is my daughter's life we're talking about. I couldn't tell you. I don't want her taken from me."

Trenton's eyes hardened on hers. "And why would I do that?"

Ginny shook her head. "Not you. Gideon."

"Ginny, tell me you didn't kidnap her."

Ginny rubbed fresh tears. "I can't."

Trenton rose and slammed a fist on the table. "Dammit, Ginny."

Ginny rose, anger now a fire in her belly. "Don't you yell at me. She would have died in the fire if I hadn't taken her. I was running from my parents' house when I found my husband Daniel lying in the grass. He was covered in burns and crying for me to help. But I kept running. I grabbed Levi from where he was hiding. He was terrified, but he stayed with me. We tried to find our sister. But she was gone. So was her husband. I found Gwenny in her crib screaming. The house was close to the warehouse, and it had caught fire. I made Levi grab as much stuff as he could, and I wrapped Gwenny up in her bedding. And we just kept running."

Trenton turned back to face her. "Did you try to find

your sister?"

Ginny hesitated but then shook her head. "No. Eventually the police did, but what was there to find? Most of the cult's records were also stored in that warehouse. That included birth certificates, and who knows what else. But it didn't matter. I couldn't give her back. I just couldn't. Thankfully, Levi was eighteen by the time we ran."

Trenton ran a hand through his hair. "What a cluster."

"But I have temporary custody now. The lawyer who helped me is also helping me with Gwenny. There is a hearing in two months and the judge is going to finalize the adoption. No one will ever find her mother, Trenton. She was too brainwashed. And I couldn't let Gwenny go back to the cult. I couldn't let her live the same life I did. But if it makes you feel better, she knows I'm not her real mother."

Trenton started pacing. "Could the man in black be her father?"

Ginny had wondered about that herself. "I don't think so. He wants her, though. But I can't figure out why. When I refused to tell him where she was, he threatened to call the cops and tell them I kidnapped her. He then tried to beat her location out of me. If he were her father, why the games? If he were her father, he'd have every right to go to the cops and claim her as his. He'd have the right to take her from me."

Trenton stopped. "Hell, it's no wonder you don't trust cops. Between the ones that tried to kill you, the ones that didn't investigate the fire, and the ones you fear will take Gwenny from you. But Ginny, Gideon won't and can't take her from you if you have legal rights to her."

"But what if the man in black told the police I kidnapped her? Papers or not, they would take her until it was sorted out. Trenton, I'm sorry. I'm sorry for the lies. I'm sorry for keeping the truth from you. But I'm not sorry about Gwenny; I'm protecting her the best I know how. And the fewer people who know about her, the better. My boss doesn't know about her. Neither does my agent."

"What about when you were arrested? Did they take Gwenny?"

Ginny swallowed and nodded. "For two weeks. Remember the lawyer who helped me? She helped me get Gwenny back. She found a judge who was willing to see me. The judge granted me temporary custody. I was already caring for her, and she was sympathetic to what happened. She's the one who will hand down the final verdict if I can adopt her."

Trenton swore. Then he turned back to her. "Levi is your brother, right?"

Ginny gave him a small smile. "Yes. But I guess there's something I should tell you about him."

"It can't be any worse than some of the other things you've told me since we met."

"I guess that depends. After he was born and some time passed, we could tell there was something different about him. He didn't talk as well as the kids his age; he didn't crawl or walk when other kids did. And when he started school, he couldn't keep up with the other kids. My father would tell him he was stupid. That he was no son of his. But he's not stupid. He's just different. He thinks differently than other people. I helped raise him until I was forced to marry Daniel. Daniel did let him come to visit and to stay sometimes. But I knew my dad was going to throw him out. That's when I started plotting."

"To leave the cult?"

Ginny shook her head as she sat back down. "Not just leave it. Destroy it. And I wasn't the only one. There were a lot of women who wanted out. But I was ultimately responsible for the fire."

Trenton started pacing again. "I knew there was more to the story. What did you do?"

"I didn't want to be a wife. Or a mother. I wanted to be free. The women and I would meet in secret while our husbands were gone. We were plotting against the cult. We knew we had to do this together. If only one of us rebelled, we would have been killed. But we thought they couldn't kill us all. We were wrong. The police I told you about had accused me of kidnapping my brother. I had hidden him so my father couldn't find him. The two officers led the men who were going to make an example of us. That's why they were shooting. And that's why the fire broke out and why people were killed."

Trenton thought back to what she had told him before. "You said you know who killed the cop. Was it Levi?"

"Levi would never hurt anyone. My mother killed him. The officer had come to my parents' house looking for me. When he couldn't find me, he assaulted my mom. I don't know where she found the courage, but when he slammed her up against the kitchen counter to rape her, she grabbed the knife she'd been using. She somehow managed to stab it into his side. She hit his liver, and he bled out on the kitchen floor. I found her crying over the body. She told me what happened. She said my father was going to kill her when he found out. She told me to run. So I did."

She took a deep breath. "The fire broke out when one of the women threw a bomb from the warehouse at the warehouse. Like I said before, there was more than just food supplies there. The other munitions blew up and a huge explosion threw the fire everywhere. At least it seemed that way. I don't know what happened after."

Trenton came to her. "Because you ran."

She closed her eyes. "Yes. I ran."

"I can't wait to meet Gwenny. Levi, too."

Ginny's eyes flew open. "What?"

Trenton lifted her to her feet and pulled her to him. "Ginny. You don't get it. I'm not going anywhere. And neither are you. You're mine."

Ginny wrapped her arms around his neck and buried her face against his throat. Tears of relief wet his skin. "I want to be yours."

"Good. Now swear to me that's everything. And mean it."

She leaned back. She held up her right hand. "I swear."

Chapter Eleven

Trenton maneuvered the boat through the headwinds. Ginny was sitting on the bench nearby, watching him. She'd helped him close the windows to keep the rain out and then settled nearby. The squall had turned into a bigger storm than predicted, but it was still just a small one.

Ginny had been quiet since she'd told him about Gwenny. Of all the things she'd told him, that had shocked him the most. But upon reflection, he could understand why. She was protecting her daughter. He couldn't fault her for that. But he couldn't say he knew much about kids. He never really gave any thought to them. Some part of him never thought to get married and have a family. When you grew up like he did, you weren't inclined to follow normal paths.

But Ginny. Well, she had him thinking all sorts of things. Like it might not be bad to be married to someone like her. She was smart, she was compassionate, and she could understand the pain that lived inside him. She knew exactly what he had lived through. And then some. He'd never been subjected to a forced marriage. Part of him still wished Daniel Hamlin were still alive so he could throttle him.

But Gwenny put a new spin on things. He'd have to think about her and what that meant to any future he might have with Ginny. But he could hear his Aunt Emily's voice in the back of his mind. She loved him; she had been the one to teach him what love was. His uncle loved him, but Trenton had been afraid of him for a long time. But his aunt had told him that family was simply those whom we choose to love. And while he knew there were plenty of people in the world who would disagree with her, he understood what she had meant. He was her son now. And he didn't need to be afraid.

Ginny was his now. And he'd figure out the rest. First step was to get to know more about her family.

Trenton spun the wheel and headed north. "So what's Gwenny's real name? I'm guessing it's not Gwendolyn."

"You'd be wrong."

Trenton turned and smiled at her. "I got one right. After Gentiana, I figured it would be something like that."

Ginny tucked her legs beneath her. "My sister wanted to call her Guinevere, like the knights of the round table. Her husband didn't like it. My sister didn't care for Gwenneth. So Gwendolyn it was."

"To be fair, Guinevere did cheat on her husband."

"I would have for you."

Trenton glanced at her. Her face was dead serious. "Cheated on your husband?"

Ginny kept her eyes on him. "Yes."

"I'm not sure how I'm supposed to take that."

Ginny wrinkled her nose. "What do you mean?"

"You know, being the other man. But it's a moot point."

Ginny's face was still serious. "Would you have slept with me if I were still married?"

Trenton thought about it. "The truth? Yes. I've never slept with another man's wife or girlfriend. But you do make a man want to break the rules. I would have demanded that you divorce him. Right before I ran off with you."

Ginny smiled and relaxed. "Good."

Trenton shook his head. "I don't understand you sometimes. But that's okay. I like it."

"Like what?"

Trenton left the wheel and came to her. He lifted her into his arms. "A woman of mystery."

Ginny placed her hands on his chest. "Not a woman of secrets, though."

"You don't have any more, so I can focus on the mystery part."

She stood on her toes and kissed him. "Thank you, I think."

Trenton released her and went back to the wheel. "We'll cruise north for now. We can stop off at a harbor and get your land legs back under you."

Ginny yawned. "What fun is a bed that doesn't move?"

Trenton snickered at that. "I can show you if you'd like."

Ginny yawned again. "I'd like. After a nap."

He watched as she lay down on the bench and curled up in a ball. She slept like that last night. She'd been curled up, and he enjoyed uncurling her and wrapping her around him instead. She was addictive.

* * *

It was evening when they reached Ocean City. The strip off of Maryland was a popular vacation spot and a favorite spot of Trenton's. He liked the town; he liked the energy of it. As he and Ginny wandered the streets, he wished he'd thought to bring his camera. Ginny had showered and changed, and she looked beautiful in the light of the sunset. Her hair shone with hints of red.

Ginny took a sip of her fruit smoothie as they strolled down the boardwalk. "I've never been here before. The tour book says there are miles of beaches, a theme park, and tons of places to go kayaking and take tour boats. Though I guess you don't need the tour boat."

Trenton slipped an arm around her waist. "Do you like theme parks?"

Ginny leaned into him. "I've taken Gwenny to a couple. Just small ones for kids. She loves them. She can spend a whole day being spun and twirled around. I promised her that when she's older I'll take her to a real one. Poor Levi can't handle even the kiddie coaster. But he loves the food. So he gets to eat all the junk he wants, and Gwenny gets to ride the rides. Both of them have iron stomachs."

Trenton pulled her to a stop and leaned against the metal railings. "You've built a great life for them."

Ginny's eyes dropped. "Mostly. Neither of them is happy with me right now. When the man found me and started following me and Gwenny, I didn't know what to do. I pulled Levi from the group home he was living in. Gwenny wants me to come home, and Levi wants to go home. He made friends and had a job. I tore him from it. But I needed him. Gwenny started school, and I couldn't trust her with a nanny. Not with the man following us."

Trenton slipped his arms around her. "He'll get to go home. And you'll have Gwenny back. I promise."

Ginny pulled back and scrubbed the tears from her cheeks. "I'm not going to do this. Not right now. We're having a lovely day."

"Where are they now?"

"Right now we're living in Salt Lake City. I thought it would be easier to hide in a city. I rented an apartment in the Fairpark area not far from Capitol Hill."

Trenton took a sip of her smoothie. "Gray and beige?"

Ginny laughed, as Trenton hoped she would. "Pretty much. I'd call it sparse, with one exception. Gwenny is all about blue, and she's obsessed with baby dolls. Her favorite dolls have a drawer full of clothes."

Trenton grabbed Ginny's hand and continued walking. "I don't know much about kids. Definitely not much about little girls."

Ginny squeezed his hand. "I didn't either. When I took Gwenny, I wasn't thinking beyond saving my niece. The fact that she was only six months old didn't really hit me until I was alone with her, and she was crying her eyes out. But we survived."

Trenton had been wondering about her marriage. It did seem odd to him that Ginny didn't have any biological children during her nine-year marriage. "I've been wanting to ask you. You told me you didn't want to be a wife and a mother. But you were a wife. Yet not a mother."

Ginny stiffened at his side for a moment; then he saw her take a deep breath.

"Not long after I got married, I got sick. Really sick. I had pneumonia and it wasn't getting better. My father let my mother take me to a real doctor. I refused to let my mom come in with me. I asked the doctor about preventing a baby. I think she knew something was wrong, and she helped me. I got a diaphragm to prevent getting pregnant. My mother didn't know what it was, nor did Daniel, not that I showed it to him. It was easy to conceal. And easy to use beforehand without him knowing."

Trenton's jaw clenched. It made him sick what she had gone through. But he couldn't help but applaud her efforts.

Ginny laid a hand on his jaw. "It wasn't as bad as you imagine. Daniel was my age, and the first few years were okay. We were like any other couple."

Trenton was half afraid he'd break a tooth; his jaw was clenched so tight. "I was too young. I'm trying to imagine taking a wife at such a young age and essentially assaulting her every night."

Ginny stopped him. "Enough. You wouldn't have done that. And who's to say your wife would have been like me. You know as well as I do that most of those girls were honored when they were chosen to be a wife. Whoever she would have been, she would have been willing. So stop it."

Trenton made an effort to unclench his jaw. "You do put things into perspective. I'm just sorry you went through what you did."

Ginny moved and kissed him. "It's over. And I'll get payback. But I think that these past few days with you have more than made up for what I went through. So let's drink this smoothie, get a bite to eat, and find that stationary bed you promised me."

Trenton wanted to, but couldn't drop it. "Would you ever get married again? You're already a mother, whether you want to be or not."

Ginny looked up at him. "I don't know. I've spent the last six years trying to survive, figure out who I am while raising Gwenny, and trying to find the last of the cult members. I haven't spent a lot of time thinking about what might come after. I just want normal. So maybe that's a husband and more children. I don't know."

Trenton nodded. "I still struggle with normal. But the quartet helps. Penny helps. And now you. Maybe we can figure out what normal means between the two of us."

Ginny wrapped her arm around his waist. "It's worth a try."

Yes, he thought. She was worth the try.

* * *

Sunlight was pouring through open windows. Ginny could just see the skyline from where she was soaking in the oversized tub. Trenton was out getting breakfast, and she thought a soak might help ease her sore muscles. She smiled and sunk lower. They had eventually made it to the bed. Trenton continued to push the boundaries of what she considered sex to be. Sex had been sometimes painful, sometimes mildly pleasant, but mostly something she avoided. After she'd left the cult, there had been men interested in her. Ginny Page garnered a lot of attention in certain circles. But the men had left her cold. And the painful moments of her last days with Daniel were forever etched in her memory.

Trenton had seen those painful memories. He had felt her response to them. But with caring and compassion, he had overcome those memories. Sex with Trenton was amazing. He was amazing. And she had done nothing but think about what he had asked her yesterday. Would she marry again? If that man were Trenton? Maybe she would.

Gwenny would like him; she was sure. Gwenny was often withdrawn, but she was sure Trenton could get her out of her shell. And wouldn't it be nice to be part of a real family?

Ginny stayed in the water until she heard the door open. "Breakfast."

Ginny smiled and toweled off. "I'll be right out."

Trenton glanced into the bathroom doorway. "You tempt a man. But get dressed and let's eat."

Ginny smiled as she got dressed. After last night, she was pretty sure they both needed a rest. She smiled at herself in the mirror. Tonight would come soon enough.

Trenton served up breakfast. Ginny shook her head as he poured syrup all over his crêpes. "Anyone tell you that you have a sugar problem? Gwenny is going to adore you."

"Isaac scolds me from time to time. Gideon, too. Nash is pragmatic. He says everyone dies from something. Why not sugar?"

Ginny took a healthy bite of her crêpes, sans the syrup. The apples inside were sweet and gooey. And delicious. "I'm going to get fat if I keep eating like this."

Trenton shrugged. "It'll look good on you. Eat up."

Ginny's brow rose at that but finished her breakfast. Well, most of it.

They were cleaning up when Trenton's phone dinged. She watched as he went and read his text. He was frowning.

"That doesn't bode well."

Trenton grabbed his laptop. "No. It was Gideon. He forwarded a file from Freya. She's been busy."

Ginny stood behind him when he sat and opened his laptop. She'd been studying DNA and genealogy for a while now, trying to hunt cult members down, so she knew what the reports were that she was looking at. "That looks like a police report."

"Familial DNA. She tied my DNA to a relative at the scene of a murder. The DNA is tied to the murder of a man named Lamar Drake, who was found dead five years ago. The DNA evidence links my DNA to the suspect's DNA. But there are no hits on the man's DNA."

Ginny leaned closer so she could see. Her contacts were in the bathroom. "Who was Lamar Drake?"

"It says he was a homeless man in Utah. Damn. Salt Lake City." Trenton continued to scroll through. "Another man was killed in the same area last year. A convenience store owner named Lucius Stafford."

Ginny leaned closer. "Did you just say Stafford?"

Trenton continued to read. "DNA match says their suspect would be my second cousin. If the man were a first cousin, then he'd be Joshua's child. But a second cousin can't be the son or daughter of Joshua. But what if Hezekiah had siblings? And the sibling or siblings were part of the cult?"

Ginny rubbed the tension in his shoulders. "What are you thinking?"

"The man in black has to be a descendant of a relative of Hezekiah. I can't believe it's a coincidence that two murders in Salt Lake City, that were committed by the same man, are not related to Hezekiah. Everything ties back to Hezekiah Stafford."

Ginny continued to lightly massage his shoulders. "That doesn't get us any closer."

Trenton laid a hand over hers to still it. "Why come after you? Or specifically, why come after Gwenny?"

"He knows I want to expose him. Gwenny can be used to hurt me."

"Who was your sister's husband? Was he part of the inner circle?"

Ginny didn't like where this was going. "He was. But the father was part of the Nichelson family. Not Stafford."

"What if you're wrong? Follow me here. Hezekiah had one son who had me. So I'm a direct descendant. Hezekiah had Joshua, too, but Joshua only had daughters. Joshua's daughters would be close to our age. But if Hezekiah had, say, a brother, and the brother had a child, then that child would be my second cousin."

Ginny's hands tightened on his skin. "Why not a sister?"

"You know the answer to that. Hezekiah would not have brought a sister. But he might bring a brother into the fold."

Ginny's head was spinning. "There is no record of Hezekiah having a brother."

Trenton agreed. "I know. But it's the only logical explanation for two murders in Salt Lake City being committed by a second cousin of mine. Your man in black is their murderer. He would have been in the city during the last five years. That's where you were. And he was hunting Gwenny."

Ginny's arms wrapped around her waist. "She's just a little girl. She's no threat."

Trenton took her into his arms. "We need to get a DNA sample from Gwenny."

Ginny wanted to scream at him. She wanted to yell and deny it. But she could remember his voice, "Where is she?" He'd asked her over and over.

Trenton brushed her tears. "We'll keep her safe. Nash knows people who can watch over her until we figure this out."

Ginny got herself under control. "You're thinking Gwenny's dad is not a Nichelson, but a Stafford. But why not my parents? What if my sister is the link back to the Stafford family?"

Trenton took her by the shoulders. "Because you're not a Stafford."

Ginny sniffled. "How can you be sure? What if we're related?"

Trenton kissed her brow. "Your DNA came back when mine did. You are not related to me. Trust me, I had some bad moments when I thought you could be my sister."

Ginny yanked away from him. She wasn't sure which of those two statements bothered her more. "You tested my DNA? And you thought I was your sister?"

Trenton gently pushed her into a chair. "Think about it. You were vague about yourself. You told me all sorts of things about me. And the cult. You had to be part of the inner circle for you to know all those things. And it occurred to me that you could be my father's daughter. How else could you know so much about Elijah?"

Ginny folded her arms over her chest. "I suppose I should be relieved we're not related. But when did you get my DNA?"

"Penny got it when you were passed out at Nash's. At the time, we figured it was the fastest route to get answers. And to make sure I wasn't wanting to sleep with my sister."

Ginny relented. "Okay, so we get Gwenny's DNA. How do we do that? And then what?"

"We can have someone from a lab do a swab."

Ginny shook her head. "No way. Levi would freak."

"Then we go to her."

Chapter Twelve

Trenton couldn't believe how nervous he was. He hadn't been this nervous when he'd met the parents of his first serious girlfriend. But meeting Gwenny and Levi was stressing him out. Ginny had insisted she go up first and then come get him when she was ready. He had been pacing the lobby of the apartment building since.

It had taken a lot of arguments to get her to agree to bring Gwenny and Levi back with them. She had argued the entire day. He knew she was scared. Hell, he was scared. He didn't want to put Gwenny and Levi in harm's way any more than she did. But Ginny admitted that the man had found Gwenny before. And after watching Ginny for who knows how many days while she was in D.C., the man knew Gwenny was not with her. The man had beaten her trying to get her to tell him where Gwenny was. Trenton had already figured that out for himself when Ginny had admitted it. What next steps might the man take trying to find Gwenny? It had been that argument that had made Ginny finally agree.

After agreeing to bring them back to D.C., Ginny had stubbornly refused to let Gwenny stay at Trenon's. The man knew she had been there. But after several more arguments, she agreed that they could stay with Nash and Penny's parents. He assured her the place was like a fortress; the safest place in D.C. But she only agreed if she stayed there, too. She said Levi would be too scared to stay with strangers without her. That was fine. All he knew was that he felt better knowing that all three of them would be safe in D.C. instead of half a country away.

They had flown into Salt Lake City International Airport from Maryland. He'd rented a slip and left his boat there. They'd gotten a flight for the next afternoon. So now he was here, terrified a little girl wouldn't like him.

Ginny came up behind him. "Ready?"

Trenton made sure his clothes were straight and his fly zipped. "Do I look ready?"

Ginny gave him a soft smile. "You look like you're about to faint. They won't bite."

Realizing he was acting like an idiot, he followed her to the elevator. Her door was at the end of the hall. When she unlocked the door, he wasn't sure what to expect. But the incredibly large man holding a curly, golden-haired girl wasn't it. He had to have at least two inches on Gideon, who was six four. He knew Levi was eight years younger than Ginny at twenty-four.

"Trenton, this is my brother, Levi. He's been taking care of Gwenny while I was gone."

Levi looked confused for a moment, but then looked at Ginny, who nodded. He held out a hand. "Nice to meet you."

Trenton took his hand in a firm shake. "Nice to meet you. Ginny has told me a lot about you."

The younger man blushed and dropped his head. Ginny didn't seem to notice.

"And the young lady there is Gwenny."

Gwenny giggled when Trenton held a hand out to her. "You're not supposed to shake girl's hands. You're supposed to kiss them. Like on TV."

Trenton obeyed. He took the girl's hand and kissed the back of it. "It's nice to meet you, too."

The girl clung to her uncle but seemed to be sizing him up. He figured he had passed the test when she wriggled out of her uncle's arms and came to stand next to Ginny.

"Mommy says you're her friend. Are you my friend, too?"

Trenton squatted down. "I'd like to be your friend. And Levi's friend."

Levi put his hands on his face. "I don't like to fly."

Ginny gave him a hug. "But you haven't been on an airplane before. Airplanes are the best because they can take you anywhere in the world."

Levi split his fingers so he could see his sister's face. "Promise?"

Ginny kissed his cheek between his fingers. "I promise."

"Okay." Levi left the room and closed the door behind him.

Ginny picked up Gwenny. "That's his room. His safe place. He's nervous about flying. I've been trying to convince him it will be fun. Gwenny, now, she can't wait to fly. Right?"

Gwenny laid her head on Ginny's shoulder. "Right. Just like a carnival ride."

Ginny set Gwenny down when she started trying to get down. "I'm going to go pack my dolls."

Ginny watched her until she was in her bedroom. "Her luggage is going to cost a fortune. I guarantee you, she's not going to leave without her dolls."

Trenton couldn't say he blamed her. Gwenny might have been a baby when she escaped the cult, but so far, her life hadn't been easy. If she wanted to pack every toy she had, then that's what they'd do. He swore at that moment he'd do anything to protect that little girl.

"How about her mommy? Is she going to pack anything else?"

Ginny glanced around the apartment. "I won't be back, will I?"

Not if he had his way. But he didn't say it out loud. "D.C. can be nice. There are some nice schools there. And I'm sure you can find a place Levi will like."

Ginny turned to him and laid her head on his chest. "I'm really scared, Trenton."

He kissed her hair. "I know. Me, too."

He almost laughed at the shock on her face. "Men can get scared, too. Especially when something important is on the line."

Gwenny chose that moment to come back. Her small backpack was overflowing with doll clothes, and she had two dolls clutched to her chest. "Are you going to be my daddy?"

From the mouths of babes, Trenton thought. And he had no idea how to answer that. Thankfully Ginny stepped in.

"What makes you ask that?"

Gwenny clutched her dolls tighter. "My friend at school just got a new daddy. And you're hugging Trenton. So is he?"

"Getting a new daddy takes time. We'll have to wait and see."

Gwenny pouted. "But I don't have one, so why do I have to wait?"

Ginny tweaked her nose and Gwenny giggled. "Because you do. Are Patty and Patty ready to go?"

Gwenny jumped up and down. "Yep."

"Is Gwenny ready to go?"

Gwenny shook her head and ran back to her bedroom.

Ginny turned to look at Trenton. "Are you sure you're ready for this?"

Trenton smiled. The little girl was a charmer. "Ready or not, right?"

Ginny took a serious turn. "Be sure, Trenton. She's a little girl. She's been through a lot. She'll get attached to you. Just like her mother."

Trenton swallowed a painful lump. He was wading into new territory. He knew Ginny was right. Their affair was still new. And under normal circumstances, she wouldn't have let him anywhere near her family. Not yet. But their relationship seemed to be set to full steam ahead. "Screw it. Ginny, will you marry me?"

Trenton could have laughed. She looked like a trout. Her mouth was moving, but not a word came out. She held up her hands and then dropped them at her side.

Trenton walked the few steps to her. He took her face in his hands. He set his mouth on hers. "You said you were mine. Let's make it official."

Ginny felt her tears on his lips and hers. "You have lost

your mind."

If it weren't for the fact that Ginny's family was in the other rooms, he'd have pulled her to the floor and shown her he hadn't. But this would have to do. "In two months, you'll legally be Gwenny's mom. We can fly back here for the hearing. And then once the papers are signed, we can get married."

"My head is spinning."

Trenton kissed her again and let her go. He knew he was pushing her. "Just think about it. One day you'll love me. And the past will be put to rest for good. And you won't have to be afraid anymore. And then you can marry me. Okay?"

Ginny pressed a hand to her belly. "Okay."

Trenton rocked back on his heels. "Okay."

Ginny laughed. "That has to be the oddest proposal on the books."

"Cut a guy some slack. I've never asked anyone to marry me before."

Ginny frowned. "Never? You know you're thirty-six, right?"

Trenton took her hand. "Which room is yours? We need to pack your stuff. Then I assume you'll need to repack Gwenny's."

Ginny led him to her room. "You didn't answer my question."

Trenton took a seat. He doubted he'd be much use. The room was small and didn't allow for two people to maneuver well in it. "My illustrious past with women is a figment of the society paper's imagination. I don't date that much. Like you, it was hard when I got out of the cult. The kids thought I was weird. I was small for my age, and I didn't fit in. Girls were the worst. Every girl I asked out turned me down. Then Gideon got me into sports and going to the gym. Gideon is a firm believer in being able to defend yourself. Then the girls started coming around. But by then, I was jaded. I didn't want anything to do with them. And I guess I've been repeating that pattern for a lot of years."

Ginny sat beside him. "Being an outsider isn't easy. And you were just a kid and had seen so much evil. I think it marks you in a way."

"It does. And people around you don't understand what it is about you that sets you apart."

Ginny rubbed her palms on her knees. "I can see why some people would be drawn to cults. But it's the worst kind of manipulation."

"And we're going to put this one to bed."

* * *

"Trenton." Victoria Camhion hugged him before he'd barely gotten inside.

"You look beautiful, as always."

"And you flatter me, as always."

Trenton released her.

"Jeez, Mom, let them get inside first." Penny ushered the trio inside. Penny had met them at the airport with a booster seat for Gwenny in tow.

Trenton closed the door behind them.

Victoria took Ginny's hand. "It's so nice to meet you, dear. Any friend of Trenton's is a friend of ours."

Before Ginny could respond, Gwenny looked up at the woman. "You're pretty. Are you Trenton's mom?"

Victoria laughed and picked the girl up. "Nope. I guess I'm like an aunt. And I hear you're going to stay with us for a little while."

Ginny put her arm through Levi's. "This is my brother, Levi, and my daughter Gwenny. We're grateful you're letting us stay here."

Mindful of children's ears, Victoria simply hiked Gwenny higher on her hip and gave Gwenny her full attention. "I have the perfect bedroom for you. It was Penny's room when she lived here. And I bet there are toys hidden somewhere for you to play with."

An older man with steel gray hair came into the foyer. "Trenton."

"Eldridge." He gave the man a big hug. "Everything all set?"

"All set. No one is getting anywhere near this property without permission."

Trenton introduced them. "Eldridge, this is Ginny Page. And her brother Levi, and her daughter Gwenny."

Levi held a hand out. "Nice to meet you."

Eldridge took it. "Nice firm handshake. No doubt Victoria has the perfect room for you, too. Why don't I take you all upstairs to settle in? Then Trenton can show you around."

Ginny had to urge Levi inside and to follow. Trenton could tell Levi was nervous and trying not to show it. But he'd done well on the airplane surrounded by strangers. And Trenton had explained to Victoria the situation. He could tell she was trying to be sensitive to Levi's needs.

Trenton let Ginny lead Levi upstairs. Eldridge pointed to the first room. "This will be your room, Levi. Gwenny is right next door, and Ginny will be right across the hall. And if either Ginny or Gwenny gets scared, there is a pull-out bed in both rooms you can sleep in, so they won't be scared."

Trenton could have kissed the man but clasped his shoulder instead. He turned to Penny's room where Victoria was showing Gwenny the room. "I can hear giggling already."

Eldridge led the way. "I give it maybe six months before Victoria starts asking when Penny is going to give us grandchildren. She's been glowing all day, getting things ready for the girl to come."

Ginny trailed behind the men. When she went around them, she could see that Gwenny was already knee-deep in toys.

"Look, Mommy. Patty and Patty have a new friend. Her name is Tammy."

Ginny tugged Levi into the room with her. She sat down with Gwenny, and Levi did the same. "Tammy, huh? Who named her?"

Gwenny giggled. "I did. Victoria said I could give her a name."

Trenton came and gazed down at them. "I think Patty and Patty will be very happy to have a new friend."

Eldridge nudged him. "Are you staying? Nash's room is

empty."

"I was thinking it might be a good idea. At least until everyone settles in."

Victoria beamed. "Wonderful. I'll have dinner done in an hour. How does spaghetti sound?"

Gwenny clapped her hands. "My favorite."

Victoria kissed her cheek. "A little bird told me."

* * *

Ginny was lying in her borrowed bed. The Camhions had been wonderful. Gwenny was already in love with "Aunt Vicky." And Eldridge had been kind. He treated her brother like a man instead of someone with a disability. Eldridge had spent over an hour patiently teaching him how to play checkers. Ginny could have cried when Levi beamed at the older man when he won his first game. Eldridge had chuckled and told him he'd finally found a worthy opponent.

Gwenny had not wanted to go to bed. After her bath, she'd been bouncing on the bed and singing her favorite songs. It had taken Ginny two bedtime stories and her favorite lullaby to get her to sleep. She had peeked in on Levi, but he had been sitting on the bed, staring. Then he had opted to take the pull-out bed in Gwenny's room. Just in case she got scared. She helped settle him in before heading to bed.

Ginny rolled onto her side. It had been a long day. But a good day, too. She was so happy to have her family back. There were security cameras, motion sensors, and armed guards surrounding the property. Trenton was right. The place was a fortress. But the Camhion family had learned the hard way that security wasn't to be taken for granted. Between a murdered father and a kidnapped daughter, the Camhions had lived through a lot.

She rolled over to her other side when she heard a tap at her door. She smiled when Trenton came in. "Sneaking into a lady's bedroom. Have you no shame?"

Trenton locked the door behind him. "None."

Ginny sat up and pulled the covers back. She watched as he stripped and threw a condom at her. She caught it. "Do I get to do the honors?"

Trenton came down on top of her. "If you'd like. I've been listening and waiting for the past hour to see if anyone was going to wake up. But it looks like Gwenny and Levi are sound asleep."

Ginny wriggled and tried to get her nightgown up over her hips. "Did you check on them? That's so sweet."

Trenton helped her strip the gown off. His hand went immediately to her breast. "Not sweet. Self-preservation. It's been too long since I've had you."

Ginny opened her thighs. "It was only one night."

Trenton's hand found her core. He found what he was looking for. He then bit her lip. "One night too many."

Ginny arched under him. "You can keep doing that."

Trenton obeyed. In the end, he donned the condom. "Ready for me?"

Ginny panted. "You tell me."

Trenton anchored her hips and slowly sealed their bodies together.

Ginny was very conscious that there was a little girl across the hall and her brother. She bit his ear to keep from making any more noise than she already was.

Trenton buried his lips in her hair and quickened his pace. She felt his fingers once again between her thighs, and she convulsed beneath him at the touch of his fingers. He quickly followed.

Ginny smiled when he rested his damp forehead on her chest and palmed her breast. "That was nice. And very fast."

Trenton squeezed her nipple. "I am so glad you started with the nice part. Believe you me, I have never made love to a mother before."

They lay that way for a while, enjoying the aftermath. Trenton eventually rolled off and settled beside her. "I should probably get dressed and go back to my room."

Considering his hand was once again covering her breast, he didn't seem to be motivated to do so. "Get dressed anyway."

Neither of them moved to get out of the bed. Ginny traced the wings of his phoenix.

Trenton propped himself up on his elbow. He laid his thumb on her scar. "Ever think about covering this up? I could have Gideon draw you some gentiana flowers."

Ginny looked where his thumb lay. "I never gave it much thought. But I did worry about having to explain it one day."

Trenton kissed her. "You don't have to explain to me. And you don't have to cover it up for me. But I covered mine the day I turned eighteen. I felt like I was getting a second chance. I never did have to explain the brand to a woman. They just thought the bird was sexy."

Ginny pushed him over so she could lie on his chest. "It's because your chest is sexy. Not the bird."

Trenton pulled her thighs around his waist. "You're ruining my good intentions to leave."

Ginny balanced and managed to get a hold of his jeans. "I know you put another one in here."

Trenton groaned as her naked flesh slid against his. "Left pocket."

Ginny rolled the old one off and took a minute to roll the new one on. She moaned when she took him inside her. She leaned down. "I can be fast, too."

* * *

Trenton knew they would have to face his friends eventually. Gideon said Freya had some new data to share, and they all agreed to meet at Nash's.

Ginny kept fussing with her skirt. He smacked her hand. "You look fine. They're not going to bite your head off."

Ginny tugged one last time. "Two seconds after they look at us, they're going to know we're sleeping together. And not only that, you asked me to marry you. And I have a daughter they don't know anything about. Excuse me if I'm nervous."

Trenton kissed her. "You're cute."

Gideon opened the door. "I knew it. I hope you did what I told you to do."

Trenton kissed Ginny again, then lightly slapped Gideon

on the cheek. "Sure did."

Ginny eyed the men. "Do I even want to know?"

Trenton kissed her again. "Nope."

"Ah, hell." Isaac adjusted his glasses. "I knew it."

Ginny put her hands on her hips. "Yes. I am having sex with your friend. Lots of it. And great sex, too. Get over it."

Nash snickered from the corner. Lilah was behind him, trying to hide her smile.

Penny beamed. "I'm so glad. Come in."

Trenton just stared at her. "Damn, you're hot."

Ginny shoved past him. "Shut up."

Trenton smiled and closed the door behind them.

Gideon led them all upstairs to what Nash called the board room. It was just a really big table and lots of chairs. He shared his laptop screen on the large TV that hung on the back wall. "Freya has been digging. We know the guy Ginny is looking for is likely the same guy the police in Salt Lake City are looking for. Way too coincidental that it's two different men. We know this man is not a direct descendant of Hezekiah Stafford, but a descendant of an unknown sibling of Hezekiah. Trenton is the only direct descendant out there that anyone knows exists. I wouldn't be surprised if the daughters don't know who their father is."

Penny shuddered in revulsion. "It makes me sick to think about how many women he raped and got pregnant."

Gideon laid a hand over hers. "I know. Freya started going through various databases. She found six other people in the national banks who are related to the Stafford line."

Ginny gaped. "How?"

Isaac answered her. "All the websites that people use to find out who their ancestors are. People are turning over their DNA all the time. It's a huge database of people. And because they all volunteered their DNA, and it's shared with other users on the platforms, it's available to law enforcement. But in this case, they would know they were related to each other. But they wouldn't be able to trace it back much further because we don't have Hezekiah's, Jeremiah's, or Joshua's DNA. Forensic genealogy is a fascinating field. But the sites have other documents, like birth certificates that show lineage, immigration records, land titles, and the list goes on and on."

Nash pointed to the screen. "Okay. So we know who he's not. But how do we get this guy if Trenton is his only target because he's related?"

Ginny set her hands on the table. "He might not be the only one."

Trenton saw that Ginny was near tears. "How about I tell it?"

Ginny nodded her consent.

"When Ginny left the cult, she escaped with her brother, Levi, and her sister's daughter, Gwenny. Ginny has custody of her niece and is in the process of adopting her. Ginny is the only mother Gwenny knows. But the man who is after her isn't just trying to shut Ginny up. He's trying to find Gwenny."

Five pairs of eyes turned to Ginny. She nodded. "He was stalking her. She had told me about a man in black that she'd seen at her school. I panicked. The only other person out there besides the new cult leader that I thought could be the man I was looking for was Elijah. So I set out to figure out who he was. That's how I landed on your doorstep. But when the man found me, he was trying to get me to tell him where Gwenny was. I'd die first. But I didn't put two and two together. Trenton thinks Gwenny might be one of Hezekiah's descendants, too. My sister's husband, as far as I know, was part of the Nichelson family, so it never occurred to me to question that."

Gideon flipped to the next screen. "No doubt in a community that size, there is a lot of overlap between families. We'll need Gwenny's DNA."

Trenton pulled a tube out of his jacket pocket. "Already got it."

Gideon leaned over the table to take it from him. "I'll have Freya rush this."

Penny laid a hand on her brother's. "She's a really sweet girl."

Nash's eyes narrowed. "What have you done?"

Penny lifted her palms. "Not me. But Levi and Gwenny are currently being entertained by our parents. I already warned Gideon; Mom is going to get on us about a grandchild after this. She's been playing tea party and dolls all day."

Nash steepled his fingers. "Guess there isn't a safer place to stash them."

Ginny tried a small smile. "That's how Trenton convinced me to bring them."

Nash glanced at Trenton. Then back at Ginny. "A

daughter, even if she's your niece, is a pretty big secret."

Ginny folded her arms across her chest. "If Trenton doesn't have an issue with it, then you shouldn't either."

Nash leaned back in his seat. "I might like you one day."

Ginny looked at Trenton. "I don't think you'll have a choice."

Nash nodded. "All right. What else? So maybe Gwenny is also a descendant. Which is a little odd to think the daughter of the woman you're sleeping with could be a cousin of yours."

Trenton shrugged. "As long as I'm not related to Ginny, I don't have a problem."

Nash continued. "So how does this help find this guy?"

Trenton answered. "I had surveillance cameras put in so that they could monitor my street, not just my house. He showed up at my house once; he might again. I'm thinking we do the same thing here. Consider it business as usual. Ginny Page is here to write her article and to write a book on Isaac."

Gideon pulled up a new screen. "I hate waiting. And I am not particularly crazy about using you or Ginny as bait. Which is essentially what you're suggesting we do. Just sit around and wait for the crazy man to find you. Freya also has been tracking money. We know the cult is in Utah. She's been running lists of businesses, not-for-profits, and other service businesses in the area. She's literally checking them off one by one. The cult has money. They all have money. And they don't have it sitting in tin cans buried under the ground. So she's digging for shell corporations, companies with offshore accounts, anything that doesn't add up. When she finds the money trail, we follow it to him."

Ginny laid her hands flat on the table. "You make it sound easy."

"Leg work, sweetheart. Catching the bad guys takes lots of leg work. But if you're persistent, and you know what to look for, you can find them. Especially guys like this who hide out in the open."

Trenton pointed at the screen. "What of the cult members that are still there? Originally, Hezekiah had set up shop in a rural part of Maryland. But he didn't operate like traditional cults. They operated more like a small village or town. There weren't brick walls, barbed wire, or spotlights. They never caused the locals any problems, so the police were never involved, at least not back when I was a kid. After the members fled and ended up in Utah, with the polygamists and such living out there, likely this group is viewed as another religious organization, free to do what they want so long as they don't break any laws."

Ginny continued where he left off. "It was the same in Utah. But men were always patrolling the outskirts. But you're right, many of the members stayed and rebuilt. The warehouse went up, as did a bunch of other buildings, but the town itself survived the fire. As far as I can tell, it's just a town now. The man in black doesn't live there. The people I spoke to refused to say much, but it was clear they just wanted to rebuild their lives and be left alone."

Penny interjected. "Where would he go to rebuild if the people in town don't want anything to do with him?"

Trenton pointed to the screen. "Salt Lake City. Just

because he's rebuilding the cult doesn't mean that he's doing it the same way. It would be easy to recruit in a city that size. I'm not sure how much money we're talking about, but an old church or a warehouse building is a good place to rebuild."

Gideon took some notes. "Maybe the first guy he killed was an uncooperative member, or potential member. Further DNA analysis says the Stafford that was killed was not related. And it's not like Stafford is a unique name. DNA in the case shows that only the murderer is related to Trenton. He could be going after anyone that he thinks might be related to Hezekiah Stafford."

Isaac stared at the screen. "What if this isn't about the cult? What if this is just about money? Or what if he's some kind of crazed serial killer?"

Nash stared at his friend. "Who just so happens to be related to cult members?"

Isaac looked at Ginny. "Do you have proof that the cult still exists?"

Ginny thought about it. "I know the man exists. I know he's from the cult. But I guess I don't have actual proof that the cult exists. Just the people I found rebuilding. But I'm not making him up."

Isaac lifted a hand. "I'm not saying you are. What I'm saying is that maybe this guy isn't trying to rebuild the cult. He could very well be killing anyone that he thinks might try to lay claim to what was left of it, money-wise."

Ginny looked at Trenton. "I just assumed."

Trenton saw the pain in her eyes. "It's not your fault. And exposing the cult is still our best option. No more secrets. But right now it's all conjecture."

Nash spoke. "Until we find this guy."

Chapter Thirteen

Isaac was in Nash's kitchen fixing dinner. "So, Ginny Page, huh?"

Nash and Gideon were upstairs working. Penny, Lilah, and Ginny were talking in the living room. Trenton was alone with Isaac. "I was right, you know."

Isaac sliced the green pepper in half. "I could tell. You really think she's the woman in the painting?"

Trenton snagged a strip of the pepper and munched. "All I know is that I want her like no other woman I've known. I want to marry her."

Isaac set the knife down. "You know I want to see you happy. And if she makes you happy, that's wonderful. I think you're a little loopy in the head if you think Gideon dreamed her, but aside from that, you've always had your head on straight. Do you love her?"

Trenton didn't have to think. "Yeah, I do."

"Did you tell her that?"

Trenton snagged another piece of pepper. "No."

Isaac picked the knife back up. "Did you ask her to marry you?"

"Yes."

Isaac pointed the knife at him. "And?"

Trenton stared at the knife. "Going to cut it out of me?"

Isaac went back to slicing peppers. "It's not funny."

Trenton handed Isaac a couple tomatoes. "No, but sometimes I can't help myself. She's thinking about it. She has a court date for finalizing Gwenny's adoption. And she's got a lot on her mind. Levi, he's, well, different, I guess. Ginny said he was living in a home for people like him. And she feels guilty because she pulled him out of it. And now she's feeling guilty because she's brought them to D.C."

Trenton sliced the tomatoes. "I'm guessing you talked her into it. Somehow, I can't see you living in Utah."

"No ocean."

Isaac tossed the sliced veggies into a pan. "There is that. So when she says yes, you'll stay here?"

Trenton rested his chin on his knuckles. "We haven't talked about it. But I know a great school."

Isaac laughed. "A great place to make friends."

"Best friends. So what do you think?"

"About Ginny?"

Trenton handed him the stack of fresh basil. "Who else?"

"She watches you. And you watch her. I've read her books. She's smart. You need a smart woman. She has a daughter. That one might take some getting used to."

"Do you think about having kids?"

Isaac tore up the basil and tossed it in the pan. "Sometimes. I've got two years on you. I've never been opposed to a permanent relationship. I like the idea of waking up next to the same woman every day. I think there is comfort in that. I think about what my children might look like. And growing older with the same woman and having grandchildren."

Trenton stared at his friend. "You still surprise me sometimes. I think you'd be a great dad. Little geniuses running around."

The sound of a woman clearing her throat caused them to turn. Lilah was standing in the doorway. She opened her mouth, but then nothing came out.

Trenton got to his feet. "Everything okay?"

Lilah shook her head as if to clear it. "Fine. Um, I have to go. I just wanted to say bye. And that my friends are running similar checks as Freya. But still nothing yet. I didn't want to say anything earlier. Gideon gets upset."

Trenton followed her. "I'll walk you out. And everything upsets Gideon, so don't worry about it."

Lilah turned back for a moment and looked at Isaac. Then she pointed to the pan. "Your veggies are burning."

Isaac swore as they left the room.

Trenton walked her to her car. "How much of that did you hear?"

Lilah unlocked the door. "Not sure what you mean?"

Trenton held her door open while she climbed inside. "You're a terrible liar. But I won't tell."

"Night, Trenton."

"Night." Trenton closed her car door and waited until she drove off. He glanced around. The street was quiet. But he couldn't shake the feeling that he was being watched.

He continued to stand outside, his senses alert to any movement.

Isaac came outside and stepped down from the porch. "Dinner's done."

Trenton ignored him and took a few more steps toward

the street.

In a moment, everything went crazy.

"Trenton!" Isaac shouted from the steps and ran toward him.

Trenton saw a dark figure in his peripheral vision coming out of the bushes. But before he could turn, a body slammed into him. He felt his head smack against the brick walkway as he hit the ground.

A man's howl of pain filled the quiet night.

Gideon slammed out the front door, with Nash following closely. "What the hell?"

Isaac lay on the ground, his hands covering his face. The man's large frame was curling in on itself.

"Son of a bitch!" Gideon roared and took off down the road after the dark figure.

Trenton's gaze was blurry, but he hadn't passed out. He managed to get to his knees. He saw Penny and Ginny rushing to the scene.

Nash tried to pull Isaac's hands from his face. "Get water. Lots of it. Now!"

Penny and Ginny raced back inside. Penny returned first with a gallon jug from the kitchen. "Here."

Nash was talking calmly to Isaac. "Move your hands. I've got to see."

Trenton saw puddles on the ground, and when his vision cleared enough, he could see red burns on Isaac's face. Adrenaline surging, he managed to crawl to his friend. "What happened?"

Nash shook his head while steadily pouring the water on the burns. "We need some saline or something."

Ginny handed him a large pot full of water. "I have saline solution for my contacts."

Nash simply gestured at her. "Come on, buddy. Stop fighting me."

Trenton went behind Isaac and held his arms to the grass. "It smells like ammonia."

Nash nodded. "Penny, call 911 now. Tell them our friend has been splashed with concentrated ammonia. He has burns on his face and eyes."

Gideon was swearing as he came running back. He dropped to his knees. "We've got to get these clothes off him now. Water is good. Keep it coming."

Ginny raced over, holding out the large bottle of saline solution. She uncapped it and handed it to Nash.

Gideon took out his pocketknife and cut Isaac's shirt off him. The women continued to come in and out with water.

Nash pried Isaac's eyes open. "This is going to hurt like a bitch. You need to try to stay still."

Paramedics arrived within ten minutes of the call. The family was pushed out of the way as they got to work. They came out with more saline solution and continued to flush Isaac's eyes and face. He was lifted onto the gurney, and an oxygen mask was put on.

Trenton was shaking, but he ignored the pain in his head. "I'm going with him."

Nash helped Trenton inside and joined him.

Gideon was already on the phone with his superior. Penny and Ginny watched helplessly as the ambulance pulled away.

* * *

The entire family sat in the waiting room. Trenton had been seen by a physician for the bump on his head, and his scrape cleaned. He'd cursed and argued the entire time. Guilt ate at him while they waited for the doctor. Isaac had been rushed into the emergency room and taken to the burn area. No one was allowed in.

Trenton felt tears sting his eyes. He feared for his friend. The man had been after him. There was no doubt. Had Isaac not chosen that moment to come call him to dinner, Trenton would be in the burn ward now. He should be the one there.

Trenton sat with Ginny beside him. She'd been holding his hand since they arrived. He wanted to pull away from her, but he needed what little comfort her presence gave him. He could see tears falling down her cheeks, but he just couldn't offer her comfort in return.

Trenton glanced around the room. Gideon stood in a corner with his phone plastered to his ear. Penny sat on a chair near him but let him do his job. Nash was pacing, as he was wont to do. He had been treated for mild burns on his hands from where he had come into contact with the chemical while helping Isaac.

He then noticed Lilah sitting on a chair off to the side of the group. She had her hands tucked in her lap and her head down. Every now and again, he could see a tear drop on her hands.

It didn't escape Trenton's notice that Isaac's parents were absent. No doubt they thought they had better things to do than sit and worry about their only child. Trenton could hear Isaac's dad's pedantic voice saying how worrying was a waste of time and what will be, will be.

Trenton wasn't sure how long they had sat in the waiting room before a doctor came to see them.

"Your friend has suffered chemical burns to his eyes, face, and chest. The ones on his chest are minor and will heal. I'm afraid the ones on his face are worse. And he has what we call a grade three corneal burn in one eye, and a grade one in the other. The grade one should heal, and the prognosis is good. But with a grade three, he's looking at vision impairment at best. We've got an ophthalmologist on his way to do further examinations and testing. And it's likely he'll need surgery to remove dead tissue. For now we're administering pain medication and topical antibiotics. And he's also being treated for ammonia poisoning. Between the liquid and the fumes, he absorbed a lot of it. But he should recover from that. I'm most concerned about his eye."

There was a collective gasp. Trenton stood. "What do you mean, vision impairment? Will he lose his eye?"

"Irrigation was administered at the scene of the exposure. Had he not had treatment on site, he would have. I think he has a good chance of keeping the eye, but the ophthalmologist will be able to tell you more."

Trenton's eyes burned. "Can we see him?"

The doctor shook his head. "Right now he's in a clean room that's sealed for people with burns. The risk of infection is too great. We'll keep you posted, but you won't be able to see him tonight."

Trenton's knees buckled, and Ginny jumped to his aid. "Please sit."

Nash came over and assisted.

Lilah got to her feet. "I need to go."

Penny ran after Lilah.

Trenton scrubbed his hands over his face. "This is my fault."

Nash grabbed him by the shoulders. "This is not your fault. The man to blame is the man who did it. Don't you dare take the blame."

Ginny wrapped her arms around her waist and backed away from Trenton. "I'm the one you should blame for this. I'm the one who brought this man into your life."

Nash cursed. "Just don't. Both of you. It doesn't help. I should know. I blamed myself for my grandfather's death. And I blamed myself for Gideon's injuries. Sometimes things happen that you can't control. I blame the man who killed my grandfather for his death. And for Gideon. And I blame the man who did this to Isaac. Now we find him."

Trenton pulled Ginny into his arms. "He's right. We need to find him. He's not afraid of us. But he will be."

Penny came back without Lilah.

Trenton looked up. "Is she okay?"

Penny came and wrapped her arms around Nash. "No, I don't think she is. But I have a feeling I know where she's going."

Gideon hung up and joined the group. "Freya doesn't have anything new. I hope Lilah has better luck. I assume she's headed to her friend's place to see if they found anything."

Penny released Nash and wrapped her arms around her husband. "Yeah. She thinks you don't know."

Gideon kissed the top of her head and held her closer. "I won't say anything. But I hope they do."

Trenton grabbed a tissue and wiped Ginny's face. "So now what do we do?"

Nash sat. "I'm staying. Not my first hospital vigil, but I hope like hell it's my last. You and Ginny should go. It's not safe for the two of you to be on the loose. This guy is crazy."

Gideon seconded that. "I'll walk you out. Penny can drive you home. And Penny, you had better stay there."

Penny's mouth opened to argue, but then closed it. "You'll be working all night. All right."

Gideon had his hand on his gun but kept it out of sight of anyone they passed. They made it to Penny's car without incident. "I'll call if I hear anything. And you do the same if Lilah's friends find something. She'll call you."

Trenton held the back door open for Ginny before climbing into the front seat. "Call me the second you hear anything about Isaac."

Gideon nodded, slammed the door, and knocked on the roof. The trio waited until Gideon was safely back inside.

* * *

When they arrived at Penny's parents' house, Ginny went straight upstairs to Gwenny's room. She stood in the doorway. Gwenny was curled under the quilt with her two dolls nearby. Levi was asleep on the pull-out bed facing

Gwenny.

Trenton came up behind her and set his hands on her shoulders. "They're okay."

Ginny hiccupped and spun into his arms. "I don't know what I'd do if they were hurt. But you could have been killed."

Trenton led her to her room and closed the door behind them. "I know. This guy is feeling bold. I don't want any of you leaving this house until he's caught."

Ginny stood still while Trenton undressed her and grabbed her nightgown. She then let him put it on her before dropping onto the bed. "Are you staying?"

"Yeah." Trenton stripped off his clothes, except for his boxer briefs.

Ginny pulled back the covers and covered them both when he laid down. She curled against him. "I pray Isaac is going to be okay."

Trenton went rigid for a second before relaxing. "He might be a teacher and a scholar, but he's one tough S.O.B. He'll be lecturing again in no time."

Ginny trembled against him. "I never thought he'd come after you. I was so worried about Gwenny. And I suppose myself, too. Do you think he knows who you are?"

Trenton rolled onto his side so he could see her. "Given that he came after me, I'd say it's probable. But why not just shoot me or stab me? Why the chemical attack? The man who killed in Salt Lake City used a knife. I can't figure out what he hoped to gain by attacking this way? He could have jumped me from the bushes the moment Lilah left, plunged a knife into me more than once, and fled while I bled to death."

"Ammonia." Ginny's brain clicked. She jumped from the bed and grabbed her laptop.

Trenton turned the lamp on. "What?"

"Ammonia. The warehouse. I remember one of the women who was willing to talk to me. She said her son died of ammonia poisoning during the fire in the warehouse. The warehouse was huge. It stored all sorts of supplies. Some of those supplies would be ammonia. Ammonia is used in farming. The entire group was self-sufficient, and we grew our own food. There were always people at the warehouse. My husband was one of them. My assumption was he crawled out of the building after the explosion. He was burned, and he could barely breathe. Joshua died in the building, too. The woman wasn't sure how many others. But the containers of ammonia could have exploded in the heat. She said her son died of inhalation of ammonia, not smoke."

Trenton sat up when Ginny joined him on the bed and showed him the notes she'd taken. "This interview is from almost two years ago. When did the threats start?"

Ginny tried to remember. "These were the first in-person interviews I conducted. It took me a while to settle after I left the cult. I started the preliminary research on the cult members about a year after I got out. I started researching genealogy and started going through old photos trying to piece the members together. Then honestly, I was raising Gwenny by myself and it was hard to find time to do anything else. It wasn't until she was four and started preschool that I had a little spare time. That's when I found that the members were still in Utah. The nearby town had annexed the property, so it wasn't unincorporated anymore. The warehouse was just a shell, and the nearby buildings had been demolished. But the rest of the town still existed much like it did when I left. It was shortly after I got back that I first started noticing someone following me. I thought at first it was my imagination. But then a few months later, he tried to abduct Gwenny. I spent the next year and a half moving from place to place, but I never left Salt Lake City. After he tried to abduct Gwenny a second time, that's when I set up the apartment and put Levi and Gwenny in it and decided to disappear for a time. I was watching and waiting. But the man didn't show. Then I started laying a trail for him to find me. I saw him a couple of times before I found you, so I thought he might have followed me. But I couldn't be sure, and I knew I had to see if you were the man. But I knew the moment we met you weren't."

Trenton took the laptop and continued reading. "What if he lived there two years ago? What if he saw you and learned what you were asking folks? And he didn't like the questions. Or it stirred up memories. You could have been a trigger."

Ginny didn't like the sound of that. "I didn't keep my presence a secret. Many people refused to talk to me. But I was persistent and found a few. What if he's one of the people I talked to?"

Trenton pulled up the faces. "It could be. That could be why he hides his face from you. What if you could identify him?"

Ginny watched while Trenton grabbed his phone. She read the group text he sent to Gideon and Lilah. "You're going to have them investigate all the people who live there?"

Trenton closed the laptop and set it on the side table. "People past and present. It's better than the alternative, which is to just wait until he shows up again."

Ginny lay down when Trenton did. She stared at the ceiling. Her mind was spinning a mile a minute. She had talked to so many people. Most refused to say much back, but it was possible the man in black was someone she met. If rebuilding the cult was not the man's purpose, then what was it?

Trenton brushed a strand of hair from her cheek. "We should sleep. Gideon says the best way to do that when your mind doesn't want to is to think of all the good things. He says to think about the people you love and those who love you. To know that everything you do and everything you are is because of them."

Ginny turned her head. "I love Gwenny. And I love Levi. And for better or worse, I love you."

Trenton pulled her closer and kissed her. "I love you, Ginny."

Ginny returned the kiss. She opened her mouth to his and rolled until she was on her back and Trenton was on top of her. She kissed him as she slid his briefs down past his hips. She opened her thighs to him as he lifted her nightgown. He fumbled for the condom in the nightstand.

"Not today, but one day, Ginny, we'll add to our family."

Family. Yes, that is what they were now. She knew he

was right. One day they would add to their family. And she looked forward to that day.

Chapter Fourteen

Trenton and Ginny were eating breakfast with Gwenny and Levi when Lilah rushed into the room.

"Thank goodness Penny was here. I didn't think I would get in." Lilah came to a halt. Her eyes widened as she looked at the little girl. "I'm sorry, I forgot. I've got something."

Trenton rose but kept a hand on Ginny's shoulder to keep her in her seat. "We can talk in the other room. You look like you could use some coffee."

Lilah shook her head. "Too much already. I've been up all night. But I found something."

Trenton led her to the living room. "Did you drive?"

Lilah ignored the question and opened her laptop. "Last night you sent a note that you thought one of the people Ginny interviewed could be the man. So I started on the names. Men first. I didn't get a hit. But then I found a woman name Katherine. She lost her son in the fire. Ginny's notes said her son died from ammonia exposure. That he'd been burned and poisoned by it. So I called Freya. She has been compiling DNA records and tracing different people's family lines. We were both shocked. It was so easy to find once we knew what we were looking for."

Trenton tamped down his impatience. "What was easy to find?"

Lilah pulled up the file Ginny had created on the family lineage. "In the pictures she took that were in the archives that Joshua kept, there was a picture of a man named Cyrus. So then I got to thinking, within the archives, Joshua had a picture of Hezekiah, Jeremiah, and himself. But why did he have a picture of a man named Cyrus? You two said you thought Hezekiah might have had a brother. That's how the man in black would be your second cousin. So, I took the picture of this unknown man and had Freya dig into the files she's been compiling. But while I was digging into Katherine, married last name Connor, within her profile she uploaded a lot of her family's history. One of the pictures she loaded was of a man named Cyrus. She said Cyrus was her dad. And guess whose picture it matched? It matched the photo that Ginny had from Joshua's files. So Cyrus is the father of the woman, Katherine, who had your cousin. Working backward, Cyrus is Hezekiah's brother. Then in her profile, Katherine put that she had two sons. One was deceased, her son John. She posted his death certificate. Ammonia poisoning. And she listed another son. His name is Luke. She didn't load a DNA profile for him, but I would bet money Luke's DNA will match the DNA the cops have on file for their Salt Lake City killer."

Trenton grabbed her shoulders and impulsively kissed her. "You did it."

Lilah blushed. "Ginny put me on the path. Freya is going to reach out to Gideon."

Ginny cleared her throat and looked at a blushing Lilah. "Are you leaving?"

Lilah grabbed her laptop. "Mom has a doctor's

appointment. I need to go. I emailed you what I found. Freya has my files, and she's compiling hers and mine for Gideon and will send them over. Then it's a matter of an arrest warrant and sharing with the Salt Lake City police. Freya already chatted with their homicide department."

Trenton hugged her. "Thank you, Lilah."

Lilah hitched her bag over her shoulder. "Any word on Isaac yet?"

Trenton released her. "Just that he's stable. We should know more this afternoon."

Lilah nodded and left.

Ginny watched her go. "I can't believe she might have found him."

Trenton held out his hand. "Now it's up to Gideon. I should go check on Isaac. I want you to stay here. You'll be safer behind these walls."

Ginny took his hand. "So will you. But you won't stay."

"Isaac is my closest friend. I want to be the first person he sees."

Ginny released him. "Okay. I'll stay here. I'm sure Victoria has plenty of activities planned for today. I'll join in."

Trenton lightly kissed her. "I'll be back."

* * *

Trenton spent the day at the hospital. Isaac was moved out of the burn ward and into a regular hospital room. Minus the burns, the doctor said he was otherwise stable. It took everything in him not to gasp when he finally got to see him.

Isaac was still as he lay on the hospital bed. He had an IV, and his eyes looked like they were weeping. Swallowing a lump in his throat, he came to stand by Isaac's bed.

Isaac's eyes were open. His left eye was deep red and irritated, but you could see the blue iris and pupil. On his right, his once dark blue eye was covered in what looked like a white film with barely the iris of his eye showing through. The burns were worst around his right eye, both above and below.

Isaac tipped his head. "Are you okay?"

Trenton touched the undamaged skin on his cheek. "I'm fine. You saved me."

Isaac's voice was low. "You would have for me. I love you, man."

Trenton gazed at his friend, his eyes closing. The burns were just as bad on the outside. "You know I love you. Best friends for life. But I never wanted you hurt. Certainly not for me."

Isaac drifted. "You would have died. He was aiming straight for the center of your face. It would have gone up your nose and into your mouth. Had to save you."

Trenton watched the rise and fall of Isaac's chest as he fell back asleep. He took a seat. After Ginny had fallen asleep, Trenton spent the night trying to remember if he had seen anything of the attacker. But try as he might, he had only been a shadow.

Nash entered the room. His jaw clenched as he gazed at his friend. He didn't utter a word. He just took a seat. Gideon and Penny followed. Penny wept while Gideon held her. Lilah came in a while later and sat farthest away in the corner.

They all sat quietly, each with their thoughts heavy. Trenton had texted Ginny an update, and she assured him they were safe and sound.

It was much later in the evening when Isaac woke again. "I can see with my left eye. You guys are all beat. Did any of you sleep?"

Penny came and kissed him softly on the lips. "Not when our friend is hurt."

Isaac looked at his friends. "Please, go. I'm going to be okay. You need to rest. And so do I."

Gideon hugged his friend. "I'm going to drop Penny off and head to the precinct. We'll find this guy."

Nash was next. "Mom and Dad are worried. They wanted to come see you, but they're staying on lock down. I second what Gideon said. We'll find this bastard."

Lilah stayed for a little longer. She didn't move from the seat in the corner where she'd been sitting until Isaac was once again asleep. "Keep me posted."

Trenton nodded but kept his eyes on Isaac. He said one last silent prayer and headed outside. It was dark, and the parking lot didn't have many people in it. He took his time heading for his car, trying to sort out what had happened and what they had learned.

His phone rang. It was Gideon. "What's up?"

Gideon's voice held a note of satisfaction and relief. "He's been caught. Freya found him. He's been staying at the same hotel where he attacked Ginny."

Trenton found his words. "You're sure?"

Gideon's voice was clear on the line. "One hundred percent. I just arrived at the precinct, and I have to say, he's not what I expected. Luke Connor. Age thirty-five. Caucasian, which I expected. He's not a very big guy. Maybe five eight. Weighs a hundred and fifty. Black hair and blue eyes. Trenton, he's got scars on his face, like burns."

Trenton swore. "Chemical?"

Gideon replied. "I can't say for sure. I'm not an expert. Bullets and knives, maybe. But he's been in an interrogation room for less than an hour with one of our detectives, and he's already crying and confessing. When he's not confessing, he's been chanting numbers. He keeps repeating the same sequence over and over. I've sent the number to Freya and Lilah, but nothing so far."

Trenton unlocked his car. "Keep me posted."

"Will do."

Trenton hung up and tossed the phone on the passenger seat. He was about to get in his car when he heard Lilah's voice.

"Trenton?"

Trenton turned. Her eyes were full of fear. "What?"

A petite woman wearing all black came around the side of the SUV parked next to his Porsche. She had graying black hair that was scraped back from a gaunt, wrinkled face. Her brown eyes were on him as she pointed the gun she carried at Lilah. "I'm the 'what.'"

Lilah's voice was shaky. "The number. I found it. It's a tracking code. I was coming to find you."

The woman took a step closer. "And she found me

instead. I've been waiting all day, but Gentiana never left that house. And now you have my son."

"Katherine."

The older woman nodded. "We're going to go to that house Gentiana is in. And you're going to get me Gwendolyn."

Trenton didn't look at Lilah. "And why would I do that?"

"Because I'll put a bullet in your friend's head, that's why. And then yours. The way I see it, I shoot you, and Gentiana is bound to come rushing to your side. And she'll do anything for that niece of hers."

The woman shoved Lilah against the car. "Get in."

The two-door Porsche was small, and Lilah had to climb in behind the front seat. The woman held the gun on Lilah and climbed into the back with her. "Now get in and drive."

Trenton climbed in. The car started with a roar. He knew he had to wait for an opportunity to open up. He couldn't risk another friend getting hurt because of him. He drove the speed limit to the Camhion's house.

"Now open the gate and tell that guard we're friends."

Trenton punched in the code but followed it with the panic code. Everyone inside would know something was wrong. The gates swung open and closed behind him. He pulled up to the circular driveway. He saw the woman's eyes focus on the house, no doubt thinking of who was inside. He smoothly reached under his seat.

"Now we go get her."

Trenton eased the gun into his pocket as he climbed out. He helped a trembling Lilah out of the seat. The woman easily slid out the other side, gun still trained on Lilah.

"Why do you want Ginny?" Lilah stumbled a little when the woman shoved her toward the door.

"I don't want Ginny. I want Gwendolyn. She's the last of Hezekiah's line. My son took out the rest."

Trenton walked but sidestepped to keep an eye on the woman and tried to keep her talking. "Who is your son's father?"

The woman pointed the gun at him. She spit on the ground. "He was no one. He wasn't part of the inner circle. My mother told me everything. She should have been Hezekiah's wife, not Sarah. Hezekiah said she wasn't worthy. And he gave her to his brother, Cyrus, instead. But my mother knew she should have been Hezekiah's wife. She was the woman who should have fathered Hezekiah's children. When I married and had a son, my mother and I vowed to destroy all of Hezekiah's offspring. My line will survive. My line will be the true descendants. Gwendolyn is the last."

Trenton took a few more steps toward the house. "But she's not the last one."

Katherine pointed the gun at his heart. "She is. We killed them."

Trenton stopped a few feet from the porch. "What about Elijah?"

Katherine's hand shook. "He's dead. Gentiana would have found him. She found all the others that I couldn't."

Lilah stumbled to a halt as the gun swung back her way. "They've been following Ginny. The number. It's a tracking number for the device she wears. They've been following her since she left the cult. Every time she found a member that was related to a Stafford, they killed them. I count four in all in the past year and a half."

Trenton looked at Lilah. "But we scanned her things."

Lilah shook her head. "But we didn't scan Ginny. It's inside her body somewhere."

Trenton swore. "That damn brand."

The woman pulled the neck of her dress to the side. She had a brand the same as his had been. "You were young. You never got implanted. But as Cyrus's granddaughter, I did. Everyone in the inner circle did. Gentiana's brand is that of the Hamlin family. But the tracker is there just the same. I made Luke memorize it. We wanted Gwendolyn to be the last."

Trenton faced her, edging his hand toward his pocket. Her gun wasn't as steady as it had been when she pointed it at Lilah. "But Gentiana did find Elijah."

"She didn't!" She swung back at Trenton, but the gun didn't move from Lilah.

Trenton pointed to the spot over his heart, and his hand slid into his pocket. "I'm Elijah. My brand is right here."

The woman screamed and pointed the gun at him. "I'll kill you!"

Trenton fired.

The woman screamed as the bullet hit her in the shoulder. She dropped to the ground, sobbing. "I'm the one."

Lilah ran to Trenton and stood behind him.

Trenton pushed her toward the front door as it opened. "Call Gideon and call the paramedics."

Ginny rushed to his side. She leaned against him as they

watched the woman crying on the ground. "Freya called. Told me what she found. I have a tracker. When I showed up in town asking questions, Katherine must have wondered if I knew where Gwenny was. She must have been elated when her son saw Gwenny was with me. They've known where we've been all this time."

Trenton hugged her to him. "Lilah had come to the same conclusion. She came to the hospital to find me, and Katherine found her and then found me."

Lilah watched the woman writhing and screaming, her voice dispassionate as she spoke. "She was using you to find the rest of the Stafford's. Freya is going further back than the last two years. She's using the genealogy sites Katherine and Luke visited to see if there are others, but every Stafford you visited that was on your list is dead. She and her son have been following you for over a year and a half."

Victoria ran out with some towels, yanking Trenton with her. "We can at least staunch the bleeding."

Trenton patted the woman down after taking the pistol that she carried. No other weapons were on her. He made no other move to help Victoria. He and Ginny watched while Victoria tried to stem the blood flow.

Gideon and other officers arrived right before the paramedics. Gideon glanced at her. "You're a better person than I am, Victoria."

"No one else is dying. Hear me?"

Gideon looked over at Trenton, his arms wrapped around Ginny. "Yes, ma'am. I hear you."

Paramedics arrived and took over for Victoria. Gideon sent two officers with the paramedics, and another officer followed.

Gideon helped Victoria up off the ground. "Let's go get you washed up."

Ginny wrapped her arms around Trenton's neck. "Is it over?"

Trenton hugged her tight as he savored the feel of her in his arms. "It's over. I think we just solved more homicides, though. We'll need to talk about it, but right now, I think you need to tell Gwenny and Levi that the man is gone."

Ginny sandwiched Trenton's face in her palms. She kissed him and whispered against his lips. "I love you, Trenton."

He pulled her toward the house. "We can tell them about our upcoming wedding, too."

Ginny tucked her arm in his. "Just as soon as the adoption is done."

* * *

Isaac was sitting up in the hospital bed. The quartet surrounded him. "It's a wild story."

Trenton leaned back in his seat. "Personally, I wouldn't have believed it if I hadn't lived it. Ginny had tracked cult members all over the country. Because Luke murdered across state lines, the FBI has stepped in. But Luke Connor was killing long before he knew about Ginny. He had killed four Staffords before Ginny started questioning members of the cult and killed the four Ginny found. Katherine had reached out to a lot of cult members through the genealogy websites and used them to track any Stafford she could find.

Turns out Gwenny's DNA shows her father was related to one of Hezekiah's offspring, just like we thought. One of Hezekiah's daughters had a son who then married Ginny's sister. The way we figure it, Katherine's mother must have been keeping track of Hezekiah's offspring and their offspring. Katherine picked up where her mother left off. Being married to Cyrus, she was part of the inner circle. Gwenny was to be the ninth and last Stafford. But Luke didn't murder just Staffords. In addition to the homeless man and the shopkeeper with the last name Stafford, they tied him to six more homicides around the country."

Nash looked up at the ceiling, his eyes a stormy gray. "Sixteen people. How many people died because of the cult? Ginny's exposé might bring others to light."

Isaac concurred. "It's not going to be pretty."

The television was on in the background. Isaac growled. "Turn that off."

Trenton glanced up. The attack on best-selling author Dr. Isaac Brandt had made the national news. Feeling much the same, he turned it off. "The story will die down."

Isaac gestured toward his cell. "I'm going to have to change my phone number. It's been ringing off the hook. I finally turned the damn thing off."

Gideon leaned forward. "How's the vision coming?"

Isaac hesitated before he answered. "Doctor says surgery on the right eye. Probably more than one. Guys, the vision isn't going to fully come back in that eye. The damage is severe. They might be able to restore some of it, but what's worse? Seeing more and it still being blurry, or barely seeing out of it at all?"

Trenton came to stand by him. "We'll stand by whatever your decision is. You always were an ugly son. The scars might help you get a date. Chicks dig scars."

The room was quiet for a moment. Then Isaac laughed. He laughed until his stomach hurt, and tears fell from his left eye.

Gideon and Nash joined in.

* * *

Ginny held Gwenny's hand while Levi followed behind them.

Gwenny tugged her hand. "Why are they laughing?"

Penny answered, tugging on her ponytail. "Trenton, no doubt. He always did know how to make Isaac laugh."

Ginny led the group into the room. "We've come with lunch."

Levi set the bags of food down. Isaac had been complaining about hospital food, and all he wanted was a bean and cheese burrito from his favorite Mexican place. Penny had volunteered to go get the food. But Ginny knew the men needed some time alone, so they had all gone.

Penny started passing out the food, starting with Isaac. "My parents should be here soon. They wanted to come earlier, but Dad had a thing. Not sure what 'thing' it could be. But he never misses out on free lunch if he can help it."

Trenton set Gwenny up at a table so she could eat her food. "It's how he stays rich."

Nash snorted at that. "Free lunches?"

"Sure." Trenton tossed a wrapped burrito at Nash.

"Steak with lots of hot sauce."

Nash opened his burrito and took a large bite. "Man, this is good."

Gideon checked to make sure his was beans and cheese. "I remember a certain person trying to sneak steak into my burrito once."

Trenton held up a hand. "That was not me."

Nash wiped his mouth. "That was so funny. You should have seen your face when you bit into that steak. It was priceless. It was even better when you blamed Trenton."

Ginny took a seat next to Gwenny. She watched her daughter, who watched these four men. Ginny understood. Men like this were not a part of their lives. Men who laughed, cried, teased, and played. Men who would stand together against anyone who might come against them. And now one of them was hers.

Ginny kissed Gwenny's brow, and they sat eating their lunch and watching the four extraordinary men.

Epilogue

The boat was filled with friends and family. Penny and Lilah had outdone themselves decorating the boat with flowers and ribbons. An archway had been erected toward the front of the boat where Ginny and Trenton would exchange vows.

Ginny was finishing up the final touches on her makeup. She wore a white, form-fitting dress that hugged her waist and hips. She'd stopped dead in her tracks when she saw the halter dress in the storefront window. It tied around the neck and looped into the bodice fabric where the ties hung down the back. It reminded her of the dress she'd seen in Gideon's drawing. And when she'd gone inside the store, it had fit like a dream.

"Mommy, are we ready yet?"

Ginny touched her daughter's cheek. "I think so. Do you have the rings in your pocket?"

Gwenny twirled in her pretty light blue dress, her golden curls bouncing around her shoulders. The full skirt hit her knees, and the bodice was beaded with tiny pearls. She'd been spinning in it all morning.

She tucked her hands inside the pocket of the dress and pulled out two wedding bands. The white gold bands were simple with no adornments, just like Ginny wanted. She didn't want flashy diamonds or gemstones. All she wanted was the simple bands. For her, they symbolized a new start and the promise of a bright future.

Ginny watched as Gwenny carefully tucked the bands back into the deep pocket. She led her outside. Levi was standing there, his dark charcoal suit fitting his large frame. She straightened his tie and kissed him on the cheek.

Levi had already moved into a new group home. And Eldridge Camhion had given him a job at his firm. Levi had a knack with numbers, and with some instruction and guidance, he was able to work at the prestigious firm, entering and processing payments from the hundreds of tenants who lived in Camhion properties. And every Tuesday night, they played checkers in Eldridge's office before Eldridge drove Levi back to the home.

"You guys ready?" Ginny lifted her skirt and ushered the two of them toward the door.

Levi took her arm as he was shown. Gwenny walked toward the arch first. Trenton leaned down and kissed her forehead. Levi walked Ginny down the makeshift aisle. Trenton took her hand from Levi's. Levi then stepped so that he could stand beside Gideon, Nash, and Isaac.

On her side, Penny and Lilah took a very excited Gwenny by the hand.

In the years to come, Ginny would remember every moment of the ceremony. The way Trenton looked in his dark suit and blue tie that matched Gwenny's dress. She'd remember the way he looked at her, and the way she looked at him. And the vows they spoke were never broken.

And then...

Isaac sat at his computer, his right eye covered with gauze and his left eye squinting at the fuzzy screen. The first surgery made him never want another one. But the scar tissue had to be removed, and the doctor told him that he needed to keep getting both eyes checked to make sure there were no complications and that the eye pressure remained in normal range. He put his glasses on, and the screen came into focus. He hadn't written a word since he'd left the hospital. For the first time in his life, the words wouldn't come.

But that wasn't his biggest problem. Shortly after his release from the hospital, he'd gotten a call from an old friend. The friend had seen him on the news. Damage control was being done, but the pictures were already out there. So far, there had been no chatter, no word that anyone might have noticed the news footage. Isaac kept telling himself that it was fine. No one would put two and two together. But some part of Isaac didn't really believe that. He'd kept a low profile for years. Even the book Ginny was writing wouldn't have pictures, at least not ones of how he looked today. Just some childhood pictures and a picture of the quartet, but not a close-up where he would be easily distinguished from other men.

He heard his front door open. Delilah. Between appointments with her mother, working at Cantwell, and playing nurse with him, she was running herself ragged. He thought he had seen her at the hospital, but that had to be wrong. She wouldn't have visited him. She was only here now because of Nash. Nash wanted some additional storylines for new content he was already designing for after the game's release. Side quests, as Nash would say, would sustain the longevity of the game. Isaac figured it was more about longevity to keep Delilah employed. Her mother had taken a bad turn two weeks ago, and Delilah had been struggling to balance work and her responsibilities. Isaac had told Nash that they had enough material, but Nash had brushed him off.

Isaac also couldn't help but feel that this was an elaborate ruse to get him and Delilah in close quarters. But Isaac could see the dark circles under her eyes. He had heard the story of the crazed woman holding a gun on her. It rocked one's world when you realized that the world is not a safe place. To know that the space you carve out to live in can be invaded at any moment. Safety was an illusion. And now Delilah was one of the unlucky ones to have that illusion shattered.

"Isaac?" Lilah's voice echoed from his entryway.

"Up here."

The slim redhead came in. She was once again in baggy overalls, overalls that got baggier by the day. He made it a point to feed her when she was here. He might only have one good eye, at least when he wore his glasses, but it was enough to see and to cook. Computer screens and television hurt his eyes, really anything with lights. But he didn't need a lot of light to cook, and he'd been spending more time in his kitchen than in his office writing.

"I picked up your dry cleaning, and your groceries will be arriving later today. Did you get any writing done?"

Isaac glanced at her. She was so beautiful to him, he

thought. And he was so damaged. "You don't have to run my errands. I've told you I can do it."

Lilah ignored him, as she usually did. "I bought you a present."

He took the bag from her. He glanced down at the box inside.

"It's software that you download. It picks up your voice and types what you say. This way you can write all you want. And then I can fix any spacing or mixed-up words. This one has great reviews, and authors love it."

Isaac held the box so he could read it. "Delilah, you shouldn't be spending money on me."

Lilah ignored that, too. "Here, I'll get it installed. Scoot over."

Isaac obeyed. He sat next to her as she leaned over his computer and installed the software. He was barely listening to her as she explained it to him. She smelled like summer roses. Her long red hair was soft against the skin of his arm. Her skin was pale, and the freckles that were scattered all over her face were oddly absent on the creamy skin of her arms. Her hands were small and capable as she worked on his laptop. He wanted to pick up her soft hand and press a kiss to her palm. Then kiss the delicate skin of her inner wrist. Then keep going until he found that luscious mouth.

But he simply sat next to her, listening to her voice, letting the sound of it soothe his frazzled senses.

The Quartet. I just love these men. As I mentioned in Falling Slowly (The Cantwell Quartet Book 1), I love video games. Even as I wrote these novels, I squeezed in some time to play. Lately, it's been mostly adventure. Nothing like saving the world from imminent destruction to get the blood pumping.

Trenton's story was one of the easier of the four to write. In the game the character is based on, he's a clone. He knows it but he hides it. Imagine what an outsider might think if he told them he was clone. Some might see his character and think nothing of it. Others might fear him or shun him for what he represents. I couldn't write a clone, so I wrote him as the son of a cultist instead. Ones' reactions could be very much the same. Thankfully Ginny cared more about his character than his lineage.

The Cantwell Quartet is centered around four men: the prince, the protector, the peacemaker, and the comedian. Not sure that is how the game writers thought of them, but that's how I do. The four men fight side by side to save the kingdom, and ultimately, the world. Each has flaws. Each has secrets and pain. And each of them does what's right. My kind of heroes!
I hesitate to name the game for two reasons. One, the books are not based on the storylines in the game, so I don't want to disappoint fans who think they're getting fan fiction, or a modern-day book version of the game. The books are my stories with my interpretation of who these men could be in modern day. And two, it's more fun to keep you guessing. But if you guess right, I'll tell you.

Also, if you enjoyed this book, or any of my other titles, please consider leaving a rating at your favorite retailer, Goodreads, and/or Bookbub. And if you have the time, a text review would be lovely. Indie authors rely on readers like you to tell others how much you enjoy their books.

Happy reading,

Books by Elizabeth Castle

Single Titles:
    Going Home
    This Kind Of Love
    Chasing Hope
    The Babe & The Librarian (novella)

The Heart's Way Series:
    For Now and Always
    Ask Me To
    Say You Love Me
    Forever Love

Bennett Family Series:
    This Time Love
    A Bride For David
(novella)

All Of Me Series:
    All Of My Days
    All Of My Nights

Cantwell Series:
    Falling Slowly
    Unraveled
    Hidden Away
    Entangled

Contemporary "Retro" Romance Series:
    Loving Jordan

Visit elizabeth-castle.com for newsletter sign up and up-to-date releases.